Puffin Books   *Editor: Kaye Webb*

THE BRUMBY

The Brumby of this story was a wild
Australian stallion, by chance born near the
home of a lonely boy and capturing his
imagination with such intensity that he could
think and dream of nothing but one day
building up a herd of sturdy silver brumbies.

But to the Australian stockmen among
whom he lived all brumbies were wild,
vicious, untamable animals fit only to be
hunted, and young Joey had to endure seeing
his beloved foal grow up into a savage outlaw
and finally a killer. Nevertheless his dream
comes true in the end, although not quite as
he'd imagined it.

This book has wonderful descriptions of
the Australian bush, and of the ways of its
men and animals. But it is powerful and
sometimes violent in the telling and best
suited to readers of ten years and over.

Cover design by Barrie Driscoll

D0813070

Mary Elwyn Patchett

The Brumby

Illustrated by Juliet McLeod

PUFFIN Books

Puffin Books : a Division of Penguin Books Ltd
Harmondsworth, Middlesex, England
Penguin Books Australia Ltd, Ringwood,
Victoria, Australia

First published by the Lutterworth Press 1958
Published in Puffin Books 1964
Reprinted 1965, 1967, 1971, 1973

Made and printed in Great Britain
by Hazell Watson & Viney Ltd
Aylesbury, Bucks
Set in Linotype Pilgrim

Contents

Part One: The Young Brumby

Spring followed a good year for the brumbies. It was not always so. Mountain peaks towered around them, the steep sides a jumble of rocks and soil. The hard surfaces and the jutting rocks of the hillsides forced them to a fleet sureness of foot that kept the unshod hooves of the wild horses sound, worn down in a way that could not happen to herds living off the lush grass and the spongy ground edging the river.

Besides, the mountain grass was sweet, the soil rich. The climb to the heights was worth it for the fragrant grass that grew among the sharp-pointed rocks. Here the short, swift storms encouraged a fresh and vigorous growth that never turned sour.

Not more than a dozen wild horses cropped the grass on the plateau and played their end-of-the-day games with each other, snaking their necks and squealing, prancing together with wildly blowing manes to nip and be nipped, and to squeal in turn. Once when the herd was bigger, their old pasture had been many miles to the south-east.

There, until eleven months before that day, their stronghold had been a wide, watered hollow in a hillside. That was their secret place until a silver Pegasus of a horse, a stranger, had come among them for a little while, like some god claiming a brief mortality. The big black brumby, Yarraman, their leader, fought the silver horse, was beaten and exiled from his herd for that brief time.

For a few days and nights the pale horse, shining with the silver fire of moonlight, ran with the herd; then, as swiftly as he had come, he was gone again.

When the black brumby recovered from the battle he had fought, he left the hiding-place in the hills with less than half of the mares following him. For months they wandered, breaking fences, chased by men on swift horses, always escaping, until at last they reached the unfenced, mountainous country to claim a free range of hundreds of miles around them. Their instinct was to choose the heights and the cover of the mountain rocks. Between the rocks the earth was packed with sweet food and the air clean in their nostrils. The vast blue bowl of the sky surrounded them, the burning sun blazed down so that they stood in the black shadows thrown by the tall rocks and drowsed away the middays.

At nightfall, when the urge was in them, they swept down the rocky hillside for the sheer joy of movement. Moonlight silvered their running bodies, giving a frosted gleam to the broad black back of their leader. They drank at the river at the foot of their mountain, or tore across the flat lands edging the water, penetrating far into the scrub country, trampling the mud at the edge of the lily-covered lagoon whose water held a strange, sharp sweetness, extracted from the growing plants.

It was wild country. Man, their enemy, worried them little, for the owners of their central mountainous strip, and of the wide, variegated landscape on either side of it, could none of them afford to fence their country in. The herd, though small, was remarkably fine physically in contrast with most brumby herds, in which the thin, harried creatures are not worth the taming.

Circling the plateau claimed by the horses was a wall of closely packed 'organ pipe' rocks of red and grey, towering upwards from the side of the mountain. In the centre of the plateau stood Yarraman, the leader. He was about sixteen hands high, a heavy, plebeian brute with an ugly head and a coarse hide. He limped a little, souvenir of his fight with the silver Pegasus. A close look would have shown scars criss-crossing the hide, where the sharp breezes blew long furrows in the hairy winter growth.

He stood in the centre of the herd, lifted his head from grazing and looked about him at the playful youngsters and at the mares. So far that spring, a couple of foals had been born, one black as its father, the other a curious slatey grey. They were not yet a week old, and there were half a dozen mares yet to foal.

The stallion threw his ugly head up and whinnied. The wind blew his unkempt forelock and long shaggy mane over his eyes and he changed position impatiently, turning his head into the wind and sniffing at it. There was no smell of danger so he dropped his head, went on feeding and appeared not to notice the movement of one of his mares. As a rule, if a mare wandered away from the herd, the big black leader trotted and wheeled and drove her back in again. He kept a close watch on his wives and none was allowed to stray – except for one thing, which he seemed to understand in an instinctive way, the birth of their foals for which he allowed the mares freedom of movement.

When a mare was about to foal she left the mob and went to some place of her own choosing, and the other horses never interfered with her.

Carrying her body with the easy swing of a mountain horse, the bay mare left the plateau and climbed towards the summit of the mountain. She was the finest looking of all the mares with her small head and the clean lines that stemmed from bloodstock.

Unlike Europe and North and South America, Australia has no indigenous horses. All breeds of horses have been imported, sometimes thoroughbreds from the finest bloodstock. In the beginning of colonization, when the great properties were unfenced, stock often went wild; all brumbies are feral.

Usually a few bad seasons and too much in-breeding produced vicious, weedy stock, not worth bothering about. Yarraman's herd was an exception. His stock had improved; the stallion who dominated the herd before Yarraman's day was of thoroughbred blood, and his progeny was as fine as anything to be found in civilized stables. Added to that, this herd had by chance always lived on good grazing and on slopes that gave them stamina and size. The sudden death of their leader, shot when some stockmen amused themselves having a 'brumby run' one Sunday, let Yarraman become master of the herd before he was three – a position he would have had to earn had the leader lived. Yarraman was no thoroughbred, but he was big, powerful, evil-tempered and a fearless leader.

The mare, whose instincts told her she was about to foal, did not take the usual way down the mountain and towards the river banks for her foal's birth. She went up the mountain, her unshod hooves sure on the hard earth, her strong legs and climbing muscles carrying her easily across the smaller rocky protuberances sticking from the earth, and she moved around big rocks set in the soil like monolithic altars.

Up and up she went; the rise became steeper so that her hooves met beneath the centre of her heavy body at every forward move, and her walking became a series of plunges. But still she went on, her soft brown eyes watching the ground, choosing the way of least difficulty. She never looked up at the splendid sight of the jagged teeth of the big red rocks seeming to pierce the fading blue of the sky. The westering sun sent the shadows of the rocks across her in long grey stripes that were grotesquely elongated.

At last she reached the top of the mountain and the steep sides fell away from her, leaving an irregular piece of flattish ground that was the very summit; a secret place, guarded and hidden by rocks that were planted feet apart when you were among them, but that looked from below as though they were bunched together forming an apex.

When she reached the top the bay mare sniffed and wove slowly among the rocks. She seemed in no hurry. In her own way she examined every inch of ground, perhaps for hidden enemies, perhaps for some more obscure reason, the reason that sent her, contrary to her kind, to go upwards where movement and exertion were difficult, and from where it might be almost impossible for a new-born foal to descend. Mares chose the banks of the river where the ground was soft and the hooves of a tiny foal need not slip, where its small body could fold itself down, and where water for the mother was near by.

This mother's least worry was water. The short, pelting showers fell frequently as though the sharp tips of the rocks pierced the clouds, and the heavy dews that fell nightly left small pools of sweet water at the bases of the rocks.

Now that the bay mare had reached the place of her choice she moved about quietly, content to wait for the moment that was drawing near to her.

The sun sank and the half-moon rose. The thin air carried an occasional squeal or a deeper grunt from the horses below her. Soon the big leader would go charging down the hillside with his mob streaming after him, leaving only the mares with foals that were too young to follow. Then when their wild gallop was at an end, usually with the first stirrings of the dawn, they would stream up the mountain again to eat and sleep through the long hot day.

Birth was an easy business for the bay mother. She was strong and active, her healthy body had never known a stable, and after a night of quiet waiting her foal was born before dawn. She licked away the membrane that covered his little body, and then with her velvet-soft nose she nudged him to his feet to nurse, whickering her soft encouragement. He stood uncertainly, his four little hooves planted wide, his silken hide marked by damp, curving patterns from his mother's tongue, and as the warm rich milk began to flow down his throat he wriggled his tiny tail in ecstasy.

The first pale rays of the sun touched the new-born foal gently and showed that his coat was a soft bluey-grey, very much the colour of the week-old foal farther down the mountain. It was a colour that was new to Yarraman's herd, a colour that was to touch several of the foals born that spring, a legacy from the beauty and grace of the silver Pegasus who had been master of the herd for a few brief days eleven months before. When the mountain wind blew partings in the baby-soft hair, the hide beneath it was Arabian black.

Joey sat on the step of the two-roomed hut where he and his father lived alone. It was not yet eight o'clock, but he had finished the milking and let the cows out to graze before he watched his father ride away.

Now the long day stretched before him. Joey's hair was bleached almost white from hatless days in the sun. He was a thin little boy, browned by sunshine, thin and muscular, for he worked hard for a seven-year-old, often struggling with jobs that were beyond his strength because he wanted to show his father that he was not afraid to tackle anything. Now as he looked into loneliness, his eyes were steady and very blue in his brown face.

Joey could remember back to when his father had come to the Children's Home in Sydney and taken him away. Jim Meehan brought Joey back with him to his bush hut. The little boy was afraid of everything then, afraid of his father; terribly afraid of the three old milkers; afraid of the big clopping hooves of the only horse. Then these fears passed; he fought them because he wanted his father to be proud of him.

Jim Meehan was proud of Joey, but he was a silent man who never said much about anything and he would have found it impossible to put into words his feelings for his son. But Joey understood, and the thought of his father had the power to warm his heart.

Life had gone hard for Jim Meehan since he took up the land on which he had built his small home. Long dry spells dwindled away his small resources. Gradually his few head of stock had to be sold until now all he owned were three milking cows and a sturdy half-draft mare. He also owned a good deal of land, but half of it was so mountainous as to be, in his own opinion, unsuitable for stock.

On either side of the rocky mountain strip were his neighbours' properties. They had fared better than Jim, but still neither of them had the money to fence his land, and without fences any stock that Jim might buy would be forever trespassing on the neighbouring land so that one man and a small boy would find it impossible to look after them.

Jim often thought about selling the place, but who would want to buy the mountainous end, or even the more cultivable part on which he had built his hut? No,

he wouldn't sell, he couldn't. As things were he and Joey
had a roof over their heads and he could earn enough
round about, fencing and well-digging, to buy them the
simple foods they could not grow.

Jim did not like leaving Joey alone all day long, but it
could not be helped. He was proud of the way his boy
took the loneliness that was always with him.

A few fowls scratched at the hard earth around Joey's
feet, the sun beat down, and always, far or near, the
cawing of the crows came to his ears. He put his rough
little hand very gently inside his pocket, drew out his
pet lizard, and began to play with it. When he had first
found the lizard it was only a couple of inches long and
it had a pinkish, almost transparent look about it. It had
been unmistakably a baby then, and Joey had taken such
good care of it and had shown such infinite patience in
taming it, that now it had no objection to being carried
about in his pockets. It had grown perhaps another
inch, and its warm little body was covered in fine grey
scales. It perched contentedly on Joey's hand, keeping
a wary eye out for the approach of a careless fly,
while he thought about what he could do to fill in the
day.

He came to his decision, stood up and went into the
hut, and put his lizard in the wire-topped box in which
he kept it. Then he went out of the door again and
walked towards the rather crazy-looking building made
of logs and bark that was at once stable, workroom, and
milking shed.

His horse was in there and Joey was very proud of his
horse, although really the poor, dilapidated old horse
was nothing to be proud of even now. Still, Joey was
entitled to some measure of pride at the improvement in
his hack since Geoff Brett of Euro Downs – the property
that ran along the east side of his father's strip of land –

had given it to him. It was an ancient brown beast, scrawny from age and past privations, but much plumper now than when it had first been given to Joey. He used to ride it slowly, with anxiety and pride, to wherever he knew it could get the best pickings, then he would throw himself down and sprawl in the shade of she-oak or eucalypt, watching while Flash munched the young grass between his worn old teeth. His name, Flash, was one of Joey's father's jokes, but Joey didn't mind. If his father chose to call the slow, bony old horse 'Flash', then Flash it was, and his small heart was full of gratitude to Geoff Brett who, instead of having the horse destroyed, had listened to his pleadings and given it to him.

Flash turned his hollow old head and nudged Joey. He was not averse to being taken out before the full heat of the day, for he had learned that such outings always ended where the grass grew sweetly. After his life of heavy toil, of cursing and saddle sores, split hooves and hunger, he enjoyed Joey's gentleness, and his light weight became something to be endured cheerfully. Flash turned his head right round so that his good eye could see what Joey was doing. He snorted as he watched the boy lift down the old bridle. Joey decided it was a pleasure-sound.

The child rode his horse carefully. He had to ride barebacked as his father was using the only saddle; but he did not mind, he was used to it. Whenever he considered the going too rough for Flash he slid to the ground.

Under his feet the sparse brown grass was powdery and prickly, but his earth-hardened soles scarcely noticed it. He could remember, not so long ago, when he had suffered agonies before his feet hardened up. He remembered, too, how gently his father had removed the splinter-like prickles from tender soles that were now like leather.

Joey rode Flash down the hill towards where a line of dark trees marked the creek-banks, passing the three cows and their calves on the way. They were the second lot of calves Joey had known. He smiled when he thought to himself how afraid he had been of those three old cows. Now he yarded them with cheerful slaps on their bony rumps, bailed them up one at a time, and putting his tow head against their flanks milked them expertly. It had not always been so.

Flash picked his way across the creek and up the bank on the other side, and they went at a solemn jog across the mile or so of flat land that led towards the steeply rising mountains, towards where a branch of the creek curved round the foot of the hills.

Joey would have been quite happy to let Flash stray towards the creek, to get off himself and lie in the shade of the she-oaks, flat on his tummy, peering into the water for the quick flash of the small brown fish, the ghostly, silvery glint of a fresh-water prawn, but it was Flash himself who jogged on to the foot of the mountain, dropped to a walk and began climbing leisurely upwards.

The first mountain they climbed hid all but the top third of the tallest mountain behind it, and that third seemed too far away to be seen as anything more than a tall shape against the sky, its sides pock-marked by the big rocks that stood out because of the black shadows that moved around as the sun, all day long, outlined one rocky shape or another, silhouetting them against the grassy soil that ascended steadily towards the apex.

It was six months since he and his father had trudged most of the way up the tallest mountain. It was a wearying climb and they went on foot because Jim used his horse only for work. Joey had been fascinated by all the strange rocky shapes about him and by the view that spread out below. Jim promised his son that one day they would climb to the very top.

Joey often thought how much he would like to remind his father about the climb they had not finished, but he said nothing about it. He knew that his father worked very hard, and that when he came home he needed the little rest he got, so Joey saved the climb so that it could be a special treat some time when his father did not have to work so hard every day.

The boy jumped from Flash's back when the going seemed steep, but he let the old horse have his head and Flash climbed slowly upwards, over the crest of the first mountain and down the other side to where the tallest mountain towered above them. Then he fell to cropping the grass and Joey sat with his back against the shady side of a rock, being careful not to crush the little plant of delicate fringed violets that grew against it, and watched Flash enjoy himself, while Joey plucked himself the sweet, juicy stem of a young grass-shoot and put it thoughtfully between his teeth.

After lounging about for a while Joey got tired of doing nothing. Although he had not been much more than a year in the bush, his eyes had developed a tracking-keenness. He rose to his feet and walked about, gazing at the ground for some evidence of the animals that might live on the mountainside. He expected to see euro tracks, those kangaroos of the heights whose powerful hind legs are not proportionally as long as those of the kangaroo of the plains. At one time, Joey had been told, the mountain had been alive with euros, and it was from this that his friend, Geoff Brett, had called his property 'Euro Downs'.

Joey found no sign of euros, but he found something that excited him even more. A few yards away from where Flash grazed the grass had been flattened and the ground beneath it was slightly disturbed. The disturbance led upwards in a wide, curving swath, and Joey squatted on his heels and brushed his hard palm back and forth across the tops of the partly risen grass so that he could see the ground better through it. There was no doubt about it, he was looking at hoof-marks, many hoof-marks, and all of them had come from unshod hooves.

He rose to his feet and left Flash munching as he followed the faint swath upwards. He went cautiously, anxious not to frighten his quarry. He was sure that horses, many horses, perhaps ten or twelve, had gone down the mountainside and up again within the last six or seven hours.

Up and up he went until the wind carried a faint whinny to his ears. He stood quite still, listening. He heard the grunts and squeals of playing horses and moved forward again. The ground fell away ahead of him, and on the lip of this fall pounding hooves had broken away the sharp edge, rounding it, and leading downwards out of sight.

Joey crept soundlessly along, keeping behind the rocks wherever he could, and finally lying on his face and pulling himself towards the rounded lip from which he overlooked a rough, rock-walled circle. In this about a dozen horses moved, and in the middle of them grazed a big black stallion.

Brumbies! Joey's heart thumped with excitement. He had heard that brumbies were weedy creatures, but this herd looked like real horses. Perhaps he and his father could fence them in and breed up a herd of the splendid beasts!

As he lay there his eyes were caught by a movement towards the top of the mountain. Something was descending slowly. He lay quite still, watching. After ten minutes he could see a fine-looking bay mare; she was coming down the mountainside, stepping carefully and slowly, descending in a series of zig-zags that reduced the steepness. Keeping just ahead of her outstretched nose was a new-born foal, not, Joey thought, more than a week old, a lovely little creature of soft, smoky grey.

The foal slipped and slid on the hard slope, often crumpling its little legs, but its mother would not let it stay down. Nudged gently, it would begin to sprawl, then get to its feet and start downwards again.

Finally mother and foal reached the flat circle of land where the horses grazed. Its legs collapsed once again, and this time she let it lie there while she herself moved quietly around it, cropping the grass.

The foal did not stay down for long. After about ten minutes it got shakily to its legs again, and began to nurse. The mother stood switching her tail, swinging her nose round now and then to touch the swelling sides of her foal with gentle affection. Joey watched entranced.

After its meal the foal had another doze. Then a second foal, a little older and more sure on its legs, came over and the bay mare looked at it placidly without shooing it away. The smallest foal scrambled up again and the two little smokies stood nose to nose, their muzzles reared upwards as if they were a pair of sea-horses that were getting acquainted.

They played their baby games, and Joey still lay on his stomach and watched them. They were on his father's mountain – his mountain; he hoped so much they would stay there.

For a few minutes Joey lay there daydreaming blissfully. In his mind his father was astride a magnificent horse completely unlike the hairy-legged half-draft that was Trixie, and he himself rode a smaller, but equally beautiful horse beside his father's – a horse that bore no outward resemblance to his dear, dilapidated Flash.

An ant nipping at his ankle brought him back to the present. He looked up at the sky and realized that he should be getting back home. He wondered how he was going to be able to wait for his father to return so that he could tell him his secret.

When Jim Meehan came home, Joey greeted him with a torrent of words, and Jim listened quietly while he unsaddled Trixie and helped Joey with the last chores of the evening, chores he had not finished because of his excitement.

Jim smiled a little as Joey's high, childish voice gabbled on about the brumbies. Jim had seen plenty of brumbies all over the country, but with very few exceptions he had not seen any that he would have cared to breed from. He did not want to dash Joey's spirits, but in his own mind he was sure there was more excitement than judgement about Joey's description of the horses.

He thought sadly that there was so little in Joey's life, so few of the things that other children took as their right. It was no wonder he was excited at seeing a herd of wild horses up the mountain and that his imagination had translated them into a herd of thoroughbreds. He put his hand on his son's shoulder as they finished the last of their jobs and walked towards the hut with Joey still talking excitedly.

They sat together on the step as they often did at the end of the day; the little boy's eager face was scarcely half-way up his tall father's arm. Jim turned his silent, seamed face and looked down at Joey's tow head.

'What would you rather do than anything else in the world, Joey?'

'Breed horses!' Joey answered promptly.

Jim sighed. 'Well, you might get your wish some day – if we ever get a few decent seasons, but right now, don't think too much about it, will you?'

'But the brumbies – the brumbies – we could breed from them?'

Jim explained patiently, 'Brumbies are wild horses, son. We have nowhere to keep them even if they were the best breeding horses in the world. Anyway, you know, it really isn't worth while breeding from brumbies.'

'But I *told* you! I told you these are different! These are big, strong horses – an' the foals – oh, you should see the smoky-grey foals, especially the tiny one I saw coming down the mountain with his mother!'

'Those foals'll probably be white if they're smoky-grey now,' Jim said, trying to steer the conversation away from the question of breeding from the brumbies. 'Why don't you give the smallest one a name? Then, if they stay around here, you can watch 'im grow up. Supposin' he turned out some good, we might rope 'im and break 'im in.'

'But would he *like* to live away from the others?'

'I don't suppose he'd like it much for a while, but he'd get used to it. They say you can get used to anything,' Jim added grimly, and then said more gently, 'Anyway you can call him yours, so you'd better give him a name. Come on, what'll it be?'

Joey thought for a while, then he said,

'You remember when that big black man came asking for tucker and you told me he was a myall, an' you said that meant "wild"?' Jim nodded and Joey went on, 'Then I'll call the biggest smoky foal "Myall", because that's what he is, a wild horse.'

'What about the others?'

'*My* foal, the one I saw coming down the mountain,

he's grey too an' you say he'll turn to white an' I know he's going to be beautiful an' strong an' swift, so I'm goin' to call him "Brumby".' Joey paused, then explained carefully, 'Because, even if the herd's all wild brumby horses, *my* Brumby'll be the wildest of the lot – so it's a sort of name like a prince, or maybe a king –'

'A title's what you mean.'

Joey nodded, and Jim said,

'Right, I see, then that's settled.' He rose and stretched his tired body. 'Come on in now, it's time we got some tucker ourselves.'

Brumby, at three weeks old, was a well-grown, vigorous foal. Since his birth, four mares from the herd had foaled and three of the new babies were bay or brown like their mothers, but the smallest and latest born, the most delicate-looking of the foals, was a smoky filly. Joey promptly called her Moonlight.

Brumby and the other youngsters played all day long when they were not eating or sleeping, but when the games became too rough for her, Moonlight the filly ran to her mother's side, peered from under her body at the other gambolling youngsters, or looked out from under the curve of her protective neck.

Within a few weeks Brumby's growth had caught up with the colt Myall, who had been born a week before he had, and these two dominated the games. Often the more enterprising of the foals would try to follow the herd when their restlessness came upon them on moonlit nights. Their mothers soon put them in their places and the big black stallion led only a remnant of the herd down the mountainside to the grazing below.

Brumby still nursed intermittently from his mother. He reached the leggy, coltish state of growth before he was seen by human eyes other than Joey's. The older horses grazed or dozed, and the foals played about as usual, unknowing that they were being watched by a man and a boy.

As he looked at their growth and wild beauty the man was astounded by it. The boy was silent and sadly disappointed when, in spite of his willingness to admit that he was seeing the finest herd of brumbies that he had ever seen, Jim Meehan saw no way in which he could make use of this fact. He had no yards in which to tame any of the wild creatures, and unless they remained at large, free to roam and find their own food, he had no money with which to buy food for captive horses. The idea just wasn't practicable and he told Joey so.

Out on the mountains Brumby and his friends went about the business of growth, of eating and sleeping and playing in the wind and sunshine.

Brumby learned very quickly to be wary of the big black stallion. Yarraman's coarse head and hide, the hairy ears and little piggy eyes filled him with respect, for although the colt was too young to rouse animosity in the stallion, Yarraman kept his whole herd disciplined in a very strict way. If a youngster came too near him he would grunt angrily, turn his head and nip a fold of hide, or give it a quick, exasperated kick from his splayed hooves. The frolicsome foals subsided at once. If Yarraman noticed an act of disobedience, such as straying too far from the body of the herd, he threw up his ugly head and trotted out of the herd, moving round the strayer, circling about and forming a compact group in the way he wished to have them. Any disobedience was punished at once and very rigorously.

Yarraman had none of the blooded beauty of some of his herd, but he was a strong, vigorous sire and while his colts might lack showring points they were still fine muscular animals. The Pegasus strain added beauty and perhaps a kind of aristocratic stamina to the herd, and it would take some years of the Yarraman blood to breed this out and to produce a more plebeian mould.

Although Brumby was unaware of it, Joey watched him continuously. He saw the hides of the foals turn from their smoky-grey to a pure, silvery whiteness, the whiteness you find at the heart of a fire. Joey took elaborate precautions so that none of the herd should ever feel themselves overlooked, but in spite of the loving watch that he kept over 'his' herd, he was powerless to prevent disaster coming to them even before Brumby had quite left his mother's side, a disaster that altered all the pattern of the colts' carefree, sunlit, play-filled days.

Lying flat on his stomach, from his look-out Joey watched the brumby herd moving about the mountains, sheltering from the harsh winds of winter in their rocky clefts, feeding on the sunny slopes when the season was good. When the grass dried out they moved to the southern side of the mountains, but always they returned to the sheltered, natural corral where Joey had first seen them.

Sometimes on moonlit nights he slipped out of his bunk, crept outside, jumped on Flash and set off for his high perch. From it he could see the moving dots that were the brumbies on the flat ground between the foot of the mountains and the river. The cracks in the earth, the dark, sighing line of trees, the stumps that stuck up here and there with an ugly, broken-toothed look were all intensely black in the white blaze of the moonlight that gave the whole scene a frosted, unreal look. Sometimes the night winds brought a squeal to his ears from the playing horses or the whistling neigh of the stallion as he called his tribe to him.

Then, before dawn, the black dots converged and Joey's blood thrilled to the pounding of hooves as the wild creatures swept towards him in a swath of living flesh, a dark stream with a core of silvery white.

Yawning, Joey made his way home. His father made no comment about his sleepy face as he went about his chores, until one morning. That day Joey yawned and forced himself manfully to get on with his chores, but finally sleep overcame him and his light head sank on to the breakfast table. Jim picked him up and laid him on his bunk to sleep it off. When he came home from work that evening he suggested that Joey had better spend a longer time in bed and less time watching his horses.

When the winter frost was in the air the colts frisked about, playing with each other, growing stronger and more agile all the time. When slowness or clumsiness results in painful nips or the thudding of hooves on sensitive hides, young animals learn quickly to be fast and wary.

In the way of the wild, that year's crop of youngsters remained to a certain degree dependent upon their mothers for longer than they would have done had they been domesticated and lived in the security that stabling and handling brings, and that gives an early emphasis to weaning. The wild mothers' instincts told them to suckle their young as long as possible, so that the youngsters, fully fed on grass and herbage, weaned themselves by imperceptible degrees, usually about the time another foal was born.

Rivalry grew between Brumby and Myall; the little filly, Moonlight, moved away from them in fear when their games turned into furious fighting from which sometimes one, sometimes the other broke away. They were well-matched. Often it was the big herd leader, Yarraman himself, who snorted his disapproval and trotted towards the fighters. That put a stop to the grunting and squealing, the flailing hooves and darting heads. Both colts instinctively feared the black mountain of a horse who instilled such strict discipline into his herd.

Yarraman usually carried a chip on his shoulder; at best he was a sullen, vicious stallion who had never quite recovered from his defeat by the silver Pegasus. Like a man who has been humiliated in front of his own household, Yarraman felt the need to emphasize his leadership, especially towards the young colts.

The time came when all the young horses born that year accompanied their elders on their wild moonlight runs down the mountainside and across the flats to whichever spot their leader chose for them to graze upon.

Growth, for the young animal, is the whole business of life, and for horses perhaps more than for most animals their size and strength depends on their environment. It is only the pure Arabian stock which, under changing circumstances, in countries vastly removed from the deserts that bred its swift ancestors of five thousand years ago, still holds to its size and characteristics wherever it is bred, on the plains and in the mountains of the rest of the world.

Even the Arabs and the Barbs are susceptible to hoof-troubles if living on soft, damp ground; they are at their soundest and best on hard, dry slopes, on mountains, and on stony ground.

Like every brumby leader worth his salt, Yarraman disappeared for a couple of days at rare intervals, and returned from his marauding journeys with new stock, always mares. Instinct worked in the herd, unblunted by man's civilizing influence and weakness. Yarraman did not know the word 'inbreeding', but he did know instinctively that a herd must have continual new blood brought to it. The herd was his business, and just as he brought new blood to it, so he trampled weakling foals to death and drove the really old as well as the maturing young stallions from his ranks.

Instinct told the mares when to let their youngsters join in the gallop down the mountain, and the leggy young things raced, sure-footed as deer. Brumby and Myall led the race as nearly as they dared, pushing ahead of the mares and the weaker foals, but keeping a respectful distance behind the thundering form of Yarraman when he forged ahead and took the lead himself. They stretched their long legs, their manes and tails streamed out, and their bodies kept a supple balance as their hooves carried them surely on their downhill flight. The rushing air filled their lungs and their bodies with vitality, and taught their hearts to take the strain of the extra oxygen pumped into their lungs by their exertions. Their hearts' high, steady beating told them that life was a splendid thing of action and surging blood.

Ahead of them the stallion drank the wind and pounded to the edge of the river, wheeled and faced the onrushing herd, mane tossing, eyes wild and head flung high as he neighed his challenge to the night.

Presently the power and surge of the galloping horses quietened around him. He waded into the water, the rest of the horses followed and the cool water slipped down their hot throats. After that they spread out and munched the sweet grass, and Brumby and the other youngsters explored round about, fascinated by things that were new in their mountain-born lives.

Moonlight whinnied softly and threw up her delicate young head. Brumby, who was grazing near, walked beside her and saw a brown, moving bundle in the grass before his nose. He whickered excitedly, threw up his head and trotted around the small object. The little thing continued to move and Brumby stamped his hooves, snaked his head and drew it in again. Two other young-sters trotted up full of curiosity and they all blew and nickered and stamped.

The echidna found this too much of a good thing and began to dig himself into the ground with fantastic swiftness, digging with his big hands beneath his body so that he sank into the earth before the astonished eyes of the yearlings until he was no more than a rough, spine-covered lozenge on the dark soil, his vulnerable underside cosily tucked into a hollow of his own making.

This strange sinking into the earth was too much for Brumby and he darted out his head, and pulled it back again with drops of blood running down the velvet of his nose. He was furious with this strange thing that had given him such a vicious bite. He squealed his rage and reared up to strike it with his sharp hooves when some instinct made him deflect the blow; his hooves came down on the soft earth and he thought for a second or two, shaking his head angrily. Then, head high, he trotted off back into the herd, pretending an air of great dis-interest in the echidna; the other foals followed him.

Like a child, Brumby loved to graze and explore to the farthest limits that Yarraman allowed for members of his herd. He was exploring a patch of high, thick grass one night when, to his great surprise, an immensely tall emu rose up in front of him. He had disturbed a father emu nesting with his brood and the two stood with the moonlight slanting down on them, Brumby glistening whitely, the emu's untidy body dull and dark, only its round eyes shining in its absurdly small head on the end of an equally absurdly long neck. The wild foal and the flightless bird looked at each other in astonishment, and then the emu began its queer drumming noise that seems to hold in its hollow throbbing some particular menace for the quietest horse. To Brumby the drumming was a sound of terror and he gave a quick neigh of fear, snorted as he threw up his head and galloped back to the herd, his mane and tail streaming into the wind.

In spite of the young Brumby's independence he still came at his mother's low whinny, and from time to time during the night he would trot to her side, just as in the daytime he liked to sleep beside her.

Before dawn the leader stopped his grazing, lifted his coarse head and called to his herd. Then he trotted forward, dropped his head, wheeled around and began circling them at a quick trot. When he had gathered them into a tight little bunch he went ahead and they started quietly back to their mountain fastness, moving with beautiful ease and power, a small but splendid herd sprinkled with little ghost-horses whose speed and elegance singled them out from the rest of the tough, plebeian strain.

The winter passed. The young horses with their hot blood and thick coats scarcely felt the piercing winds, the cold shock of the rains. They turned their rumps to the weather as the grown horses did and let the wind drive the sleet against them so that a sudden ray of moonlight turned it into a rain of diamonds.

Then it was spring again, spring, and a world that was the product of spring rain and sunshine, a world on which Brumby stamped his slender hooves and bent his head to twist his mobile lips about a bunch of sweet grass, a world that was, for all he knew, good to eat right through to the other side.

He still liked to eat and sleep near to his mother and she was placidly agreeable. When the next foal was born she would not be so welcoming.

Joey liked most of the people he knew, which was just as well as there were so few of them. He liked Bill Regan who owned the property 'Windera', on the west side of Jim Meehan's place. Bill was a hard-faced, soft-hearted man and he liked Joey, too.

Then there was Geoff Brett, owner of Euro Downs, on the east of Jim's place. Geoff was a short, stout, kindly man and Joey loved him, but he was a little nervous of Rowena, Geoff's wife. To Joey, Rowena seemed more like a man than a woman. She was tall and spare and silent, and had a grim mouth and a deeply furrowed face. She seemed very old to Joey, and it is true she was forty-five, ten years older than her husband. She dressed like a Victorian woman in long, sweeping skirts and severe bodices, screwed her hair back in a tight bun on the back of her neck and did the work of a man about the place. Rowena had, for a short time, been a schoolteacher; she had had an education and that, more than anything else, gave her a separate place in Joey's mind.

Joey did not like Albert Dugan who worked intermittently for Geoff Brett. Dugan was a coarse, sloppy man who limped slightly and had a queer twist to one of his heavy shoulders, and this, combined with other things, made him repulsive to the little boy who felt instinctively that he was cruel and a bully. However, he did not see much of Dugan, who used to work for Geoff for a few weeks, and then would go off about his own business for months at a time. No one really liked Dugan, but he was useful at times when an extra man was needed; even so, the easy-going Geoff Brett was one of the few who would employ him.

Dugan had a bad reputation for the way he treated horses, all horses. People said it was because once, when he was a young man and had been breaking in horses, he had been given a wild horse to tame, and it had thrown and then savaged him. As a result of this he had never quite recovered and that had given him his limp and his twisted body, the things about him that made Joey fear him so much. Another result had been his passionate hatred of all horses. He treated his own horses badly, overworking and underfeeding them and continually knocking them about, and no one, not even Geoff, would give him work unless he used his own horses and not theirs.

It became a daily routine for Joey to put half the milk from the three cows into the small milkcan and to ride over to Euro Downs with it every morning and give it to Mrs Brett. Geoff was having trouble with his milkers, so when Jim went off to work on another part of Geoff's run, Joey put the bridle on Flash and they set off with the milkcan gleaming in the sunlight as it rested on Joey's small thigh, in the way he had seen his father carry it.

For the first few mornings Mrs Brett silently took the can from Joey, gave him a brief word of thanks, and he turned Flash and rode slowly back home, sniffing wistfully when a hint of the good smell of hot scones floated out from the kitchen.

Then one morning Mrs Brett took the milk and smiled bleakly at him, and that frightened Joey more than her silence! But she stopped him when he went to ride away and asked him into the kitchen. Joey slid from Flash's back and hitched him to the stump before the door, doing this rather ostentatiously as if he thought that the spirited Flash might break away, and then he followed Mrs Brett's gaunt form into the kitchen. She sat him down at the table and made him a cup of rich cocoa and gave him as many hot scones with butter and honey as he could eat.

Joey sighed with satisfaction as the third scone went down. He wiped his mouth on the sleeve of his ragged shirt, thanked Mrs Brett, went solemnly out to his horse and rode away.

Jim Meehan called in at the homestead that night on his way home, wanting to borrow an axe from Geoff until he mended his own. Mrs Brett insisted that he should sit down and have a cup of tea. Jim was surprised; the silent Rowena did not often offer such courtesies. Then she began to talk about Joey.

'That's a nice kid of yours,' she said gruffly, and Jim looked at her in surprise and said nothing. She went on, 'What're you going to do about sending him to school? You'll get into trouble next year if they find out he's not getting any education?'

Jim looked worried and then shrugged his shoulders.

'What can I do? There's no school around here. I suppose I could teach him to read and write,' he went on dubiously. 'It's about all I can do myself.'

Mrs Brett nodded. 'It's hard for kids to learn anything out here. Anyway, he's young yet. I might be able to help a bit.' She turned away, obviously embarrassed and afraid that Jim might find her interfering. He said nothing, so she went on, 'I used to teach you know, before I married Geoff. I didn't do much, and I don't know a great deal myself, but I suppose I know more than Joey does.'

Jim looked at her gratefully. 'That's pretty kind of you, Missis. Joey's sort of nervous, never did have much of a chance you understand, but he's comin' along all right now. If it wouldn't be too much trouble I'd be glad to have 'im learn anythin'.'

The woman nodded. 'I'd like him to like the idea, it wouldn't be much use otherwise. Will you just leave it, don't say anything? I'll see what I can do to make him want to learn to read.'

It was some days after this talk that Jim came home one evening to find Joey waiting for him in great excitement. He ran out of the hut, his face beaming, and stood looking up at his father as Jim swung himself wearily down off Trixie's broad back.

'I've got lots of books!' Joey announced proudly. 'Lots and lots of them – come in and see!'

Jim gave his shoulder a pat. 'Give me a chance! I haven't rubbed Trixie down yet.'

Joey hovered about him while he attended to Trixie.

'It's Mrs Brett,' Joey said excitedly. 'You know their loft? Well, she said I could go up there an' take anythin' I liked an' there were lots and lots of books, all dusty, with pickshers on the covers, so I took one down – it had a picksher of two men on big white horses like Brumby's going to be, an' the horses were fightin' – an' I asked her could I have that. She said, "Yes, an' get some more, get as many as you like, they'll only get dirty up there", an' so I did an' there's pickshers of horses and dogs an' ladies in red dresses an' men with guns an' coaches an' everythin'!' He stopped for breath, and Jim led the way back to the hut.

Inside, he found an armful of books, most of them with lurid pictures decorating their paper covers.

'You have got a lot. What a pity you can't read them!'

'I know,' Joey's face fell, 'but you'll read them to me, won't you, Dad?'

Jim nodded. 'I'll try. I don't read so good, not like that. Don't you think you ought to clean them up a bit and maybe make a bookshelf?'

Joey's eyes shone. Together they found some pieces of rag and an old rubber and then Jim showed Joey how to make flour paste with which to mend the tattered covers.

Jim cooked the supper and Joey spent a blissful evening cleaning and mending his new library, admiring the spirited pictures when they appeared in far more detail after he had finished the cleaning operation.

His father watched him for a while, leaving him to do it himself, until he saw the tow head nodding between enormous bouts of yawning and they went off to bed, sleepiness overcoming Joey's bliss at the thought of all the work he would have to do on the morrow.

It was not many days after this that Joey agreed joyfully to having reading lessons from Mrs Brett. After all, a man with such a library looks pretty silly when he can't read it. The morning cakes and scones were not without their lure either, and Joey could hardly wait until it was time to pick up the milkcan and be off to the homestead.

In spite of his interest in learning to read, Joey went continually to his secret place to watch his brumby herd. He knew all the horses, all the foals, apart. He knew, if Brumby did not, that the mare, his mother, was about to foal again.

Joey gazed with apprehensive eyes at the wide strip of level land at the foot of the mountain, across which he knew that the horses thundered every night, for crossing it at several places were long, dry crevasses, none of them more than four or five feet deep, circling and twisting like the dry beds of streams. To Joey's eyes these formed a hazard which the young horses might forget. If they blundered into one at full gallop they might easily crack their legs. But Joey need not have worried, the young Pegasuses were far too surefooted and quick-eyed to be in danger of that on normal nightly runs carried out without the terror of pursuit.

Joey never ceased to mourn that lack of fencing and the lack of money with which to buy feed prevented his father from claiming such a splendid herd as his own.

The little boy soon lost his fear of the grim-faced Rowena Brett. In his heart there stirred a deep affection for this silent, mannish woman who, in her wordless way, still managed to make him feel welcome. In his lonely life he had, without knowing it, badly needed a friend. Now, strange and incongruous though it seemed, the harsh, angular woman had a place in Joey's life that was hers alone. She knew this and she valued it.

When Joey made up his mind that Rowena was to be trusted, he told her about the brumby herd. She did not disappoint him, but nodded gravely and said what a very great pity it was that none of the three of them, Geoff, Bill Regan, or his father, had the money to fence their land and to make something of such a splendid herd. Joey told her about the small and beautiful filly, Moonlight, and how splendid Brumby and Myall looked, especially when they were fighting.

'Brumby's really mine, you know,' he told her gravely. 'He's that white colour, sort of like silver paper when the sun shines on it, and he's livelier than any of the other horses, even Myall.'

'I expect his ancestors were Arabs. You know, all the fine horses in England are descended from only three Arabs.'

'How did they get the Arabs?'

'Oh, different ways, I suppose.'

'But *how*?'

'I don't really know, from Arabia I expect – except for one. I remember "The Godolphin Barb" – a Barb is an Arab from Barbary – was found by Lord Godolphin in Paris, pulling a water cart!'

'What were the names of the others?'

'One was called "The Darley Arabian", and the other "The Byerley Turk".'

Joey repeated the names and Mrs Brett knew that whatever else he forgot it would not be the names of the three Arabian stallions – nor, in fact, anything she could teach him about horses, any horses.

Joey's desire to read began with his possession of the paper-backed novels with the picture of the two fighting white horses on it, horses that reminded him of Brumby and Myall. Rowena realized that snippets of horse-lore interlarded with his lessons were to Joey what carrots are to a donkey.

She looked down at his tow head, and her grim face softened with affection. The longing for a child of her own that had been denied to her translated itself to Joey and she was a little afraid of the warmth within her bleak heart, afraid of the little boy who had broken down its defences and left its gates wide open to admit sorrow as well as joy.

Joey looked up at the kitchen clock that ticked away on the shelf opposite him, and began to wriggle down from his chair. His father was very insistent that he must watch the time and not linger over his lessons so that Mrs Brett would feel that she must ask him to stay for dinner. His head was not much above her waist and he tilted his face upwards to look into her face with his small, confiding smile. Her face no longer seemed grim and frightening to him. Now he only saw the strength and tenderness that lay behind the harsh lines, and the warmth of the smile that was for him alone. His high voice said proudly,

'I really did read three lines – all but one word – right by myself, didn't I?'

The woman smiled back at him.

'You certainly did.'

He hesitated for a moment. 'How would you *know* a horse was an Arab?' he asked.

Rowena pondered the question.

'I don't know all the points, but I've been told one thing about Arabs that might help, they say that all of them have dark skins whatever colour their hides may be.'

'Oh, I wish I could get close enough to Brumby an' Myall and Moonlight to look at their skins! I'll bet they're as black as anything!'

Rowena walked to the door with him, her rough hand resting gently on his shoulder.

'You will – if you want to badly enough. You know, you can have anything in this world that you want if you want it badly enough.'

'Then I'll have Brumby – an' Moonlight!' Joey shouted triumphantly, but Rowena looked down at him with a grave, tired face.

'Perhaps you will. It's true what I said, Joey, but there's something to add to it. You can have what you want, but you can't control the price you have to pay for it, and sometimes that makes things just not worth while.'

'I don't care what I have to pay for him, Brumby's worth *anything* to me!'

Rowena gave him the warm smile that sat so strangely on her severe face.

'I hope you will have him, Joey. I hope you'll have the whole herd, and I hope you won't have to pay too high a price for it. Now off you go home – tomorrow I'll tell you about the Lippizaners.'

Joey stopped. 'What's a "Lip-lippit-something"?' he asked.

'You go on home, you'll find out tomorrow.'

Joey scrambled on to Flash's ancient back, and Rowena waved to him and then went back into the house smiling to herself. She decided to go and get her old encyclopaedia and check up on the Lippizaners – and to look for any other horse-lore or legend that she could find to insert like bright beads into the dull chain of learning, to keep Joey's interest in the more prosaic lessons from flagging.

Joey rode homewards, hoping his father would not be late. Now that he was 'going to school' there was always so much to talk about; besides, there was a moon, and he might go up the mountain later on and watch his horses. His hard heels drummed into Flash's ribs. Flash was cheating, every now and again Joey allowed him to pick a mouthful when they passed over a nice patch of grass, but he did not like him to stop and graze, that was too much. Flash ambled on, shaking his head up and down so that the bit jingled and the earth fell away from the roots of the bunch of grass he had torn up.

They rode across the almost dry creek, over the small hill on the home side, and were making their way up the final long, yellowed slope to the hut when Joey looked up and saw that his father was already home. He was just going to cooee to him when he saw there was another man sitting on the doorstep. The pleasure left his face and he frowned. He knew that heavy, twisted-shouldered figure. It was Al Dugan. Flash moved more slowly and Joey let him idle, hoping Dugan would leave before he reached home. Dugan stood up as Joey reached the rails and slid to the ground from Flash's back.

'Hello, young 'un,' he said briefly, and Joey returned a sullen, 'Hello.' He looked quickly at his father's face. It was set and mask-like, the face of the man Joey remembered fearing when his father had first brought him back from the Home. That hard, mask-like look was seldom on Jim's face nowadays. It changed now as he looked at his son and said, 'Hello, kid', but the dark, worried look did not leave his eyes. Joey walked to his father's side and stood there. Dugan took the cigarette-butt from his mouth and spat.

'Well, I'll be gettin' along – sure you don't want to make one o' the boys? I've got three from Conway's, but Geoff and Bill Regan're workin' so I thought you might –'

'I'm workin' too,' Jim said shortly.

'Right oh. It's pretty cronk on'y 'avin' th' four of us, we should git some real good 'orses. Good thing yer don't mind – not that it'd make any difference.' There was a nasty note in Dugan's voice and Jim's thick brows drew together.

'I never said I didn't mind,' he said in a hard voice, 'an' don't get away with the idea I'm havin' this sort of thing every Sunday. I suppose one run's fair enough seein' Bob Johns has got mares among 'em, but that'll do.'

He turned his back ostentatiously and walked towards the stables, while Joey stood uncertainly where he was, an awful premonition touching his heart. Dugan muttered something and walked towards his horse, hunching his thickened shoulder angrily. He jerked the poor brute's mouth as he caught the reins, got into the saddle, brought the handle of his stockwhip down on its thin ribs and rode away. Joey ran into the shed to his father.

'What did he mean? He said, "We'll get some good horses." He's not –' His voice failed him. Jim turned from hanging his bridle on a nail. It was darkish inside the stable and Joey could not see his expression, only the gleam of his narrowed grey eyes in his brown face as he stood silent for a moment. Then, still without speaking, he put his hand on his son's shoulder and they walked outside and towards the hut. Jim's hard palm felt the small, sharp bones in the little boy's shoulder; it was like holding a young bird in his hand. Then he turned to Joey.

'Now, son, try to understand. Dugan meant what you thought he did, they're goin' to run the brumbies this Sunday.'

Joey's blue eyes blazed, he shook his father's hand from his shoulder and shouted,

'You can't let him! They're on your land, you can stop it!'

'Joey, I know how hard it is for you to understand. You heard Dugan say that Geoff and Bill aren't going with them. Neither am I. They're going to run them over their land too, and this time we'll have to let them. That big leader's been after new mares for his herd, the way brumbies always do, and he's got two of Bob Johns's mares from the other side of Conway's Flat. I can't stop Bob tryin' to get his mares back, and you heard me tell Dugan they can only have this one run. This time we'll have to let them do it, son, it's the custom, and custom's a mighty strong thing when it's based on justice. We can't deny those mares belong to Bob.'

'But they'll go for Brumby an' Moonlight an' the others —'

'I know, son, and I can't do a thing about it. If we could only fence in our land, custom'd be on our side and that herd'd become ours. We can't do that so anyone else has the right to run them and to get what horses they can. Don't look like that. I know you're thinkin' about Brumby. Well, the odds are more'n twenty to one against their gettin' him —'

'They *might* — they might get him — or Moonlight or Myall —' Joey choked.

'Yes, they might. But I'll tell you this, I don't think they will, but if they do then I promise you that I'll do anything I can to buy him for you an' I know that Geoff and Bill'd help me. Don't forget the herd've been here for a long time without havin' any trouble. They're strong and active, they won't 'ave riders to hamper them. The boys may get one or two with their ropes, but that's all.

'Four men aren't enough for a brumby run, they'll never be able to steer that mob into a dead end where they really can take them. You be thankful it's not better organized, then you would have something to worry about. Come on, be a man, Brumby's goin' to be all right.'

'They'll chase them away from the mountain.'

'They'll come back. Our mountain suits them too well to leave it just because of one run, and I promise you there'll be only one.' Jim's face was grim.

Joey wanted more than anything else to be a man in his father's eyes. His throat felt tight and his eyes burned. He swallowed quickly and his father, glancing down at his little boy's tragic face, felt his own heart contract. Why did Dugan have to do this to Joey?

'Come on, son,' he said gently, 'tell me what you learned at school today?'

Joey swallowed manfully; his voice shook a little, but he forced himself to speak. 'I learned about Arabs, they have black skins, an' tomorrow I'm goin' to learn about Lip-lipt-zers,' he finished. Jim looked puzzled.

'Well, when you know about Lip-what-have-yous, you'll know more than I do. What are they, anyway?'

'Horses, I bet,' Joey said in a tone that said that for them to be anything else would be ridiculous.

The rest of the week crawled by for Joey. He could not bring himself to speak of the brumby run even to Rowena, but she knew. She thought feverishly of all the things she could tell Joey that might hold his interest. He helped her by asking about the Lippizaners and she smiled gratefully.

'Of course. Well, they're white horses like –' She stopped, afraid to mention Brumby, but Joey filled in the name for her and she went on, 'There are about fifty Lippizaners in Vienna, all white stallions, and their ancestors came from Spain. They have lessons, just the way you do, Joey, but their lessons are called Haute École – that means High School in French – and they learn all sorts of movements and exercises.'

'Where do they go to school?'

'Why, in the most beautiful riding school in the world. It was built for them in the eighteenth century and it looks like an immense ballroom with huge, crystal chandeliers hanging from the ceiling.'

'What's those?' Joey asked, but Rowena did not correct him. She opened her old encyclopedia and showed him a far from adequate picture of the glittering beauty of the chandeliers.

'You see, the horses learn to do a kind of dancing. All the movements they make come from those that armoured knights made when they rode in tournaments hundreds of year ago – see, here are some pictures of the tournaments I found for you in this old history book. The horses learn to perform to music. Some day, if you ever go to a big circus, you might see other horses doing the same thing, but those horses you're looking at will have learned from the Lippizaners, for they were the first. The lovely white horses drink out of marble troughs, and their riders wear maroon coats and cockaded hats as they did when the Empress Maria Theresa ruled in Austria. You'll learn about Maria Theresa later on when you learn more history.'

Joey was enthralled. 'What're the horses' names?' he demanded. Mrs Brett laughed.

'Their names are very long. I can only remember the shortest one, and it's the prettiest one too, I think: it's "Florian".'

' "Florian" – that is pretty. I'll call –' He stopped, his thoughts no longer on the elegant horses of the Austrian Court, but with the herd of brumbies that roamed the wild mountains of his Australian homeland, horses that understood no more of the meaning of the word 'dressage' than did Joey himself. 'I'll call the first foal I breed "Florian",' he finished determinedly.

The rest of the week dragged along unhappily. Jim's heart mourned over his son's silent, drawn face. Joey did not complain, he did his work and made no mention of 'his' herd, but Jim had some idea of the stoicism the little boy was exercising to cover his sad heart.

Jim thought about the time he had gone to Sydney to bring Joey back with him from the Home to which he had been taken. He thought of how soft his son had seemed to him then, of how he wondered if he could ever be hardened to behave like an ordinary bush boy. In those days Joey was frightened of the big animals, terrified by the leaping, stinging insects, ill from sunburn, and his feet and hands became a mass of painful sores while his nights were made hideous by nightmares. He had hardened up since then, his mind as much as the leathery soles of his feet had adjusted itself to the conditions around him, but nothing could ever change the boy's sensitive inner nature, his horror of inflicting pain, his sympathetic loving heart. While Jim did not quite understand his own feelings about it, he knew that he was glad that Joey was as he was.

Now, for the first time since the hardening process had been completed, came the real test of Joey's manhood. Jim wished he could have spared him this; he knew that there was little he could do to help him through the black Sunday that loomed ahead of him. He supposed he could take him over to the Bretts' or down to Bill Regan's humpy and try to take his mind off what was happening to his beloved horses, but in the end Joey would have to face his misery alone, and perhaps it was better to let him do that, and to do what he could to help him when the brumby run was over and they knew the full extent of the damage.

Mrs Brett gave Joey his lessons as usual and he tried to attend to them, but suddenly his mind went to his beloved Brumby and the faraway, hurt look come into his eyes. Mrs Brett spoke to him sharply to bring him back to the present. Out of politeness he tried to eat his usual number of hot scones and to drink the cocoa she gave him, but it was an effort. Always before he had wolfed every crumb.

The brumby run was to begin soon after dawn on Sunday. The men would come from the far side of the mountain, riding as quietly as they could. If they could approach near enough without being seen, there was just a chance that even with only four men, two of them could block the opening to the great natural corral, while the other two rode among the wild horses and roped as many as possible while the terrified animals ringed about.

With this in mind, the four men, Dugan, Bob Johns, and the two Campbell boys, Frank and Tom, rode out from the little township of Conway's Flat before it was really light. They rode slowly to keep their horses fresh for galloping after the brumby herd. Dugan and Bob Johns carried ·44's across their saddles, and they were expected to be ready to shoot any of the herd that might break legs or otherwise irreparably damage themselves.

The two Campbells were the best mounted, riding rugged bush horses with speed and stamina; Bob Johns's mare was fast but not as good a stayer as the others; Dugan rode a raw-boned beast that was powerful, but underfed and over-used like all his horses.

The four men rode through the wild countryside. Long

before the sound of their voices could be carried to the sharp ears of the brumbies, they kept silent and rode along the way at an easy jog-trot, the natural pace of the bush horse. It was about an hour after dawn that they rode up the side of the big mountain.

All night Joey lay awake wide-eyed in the darkness except for an occasional fitful dropping-off into an uneasy sleep, when the darkness before the little boy's eyes was filled with pale, moving shadows. Brumby and Myall in their mock fights reared up and darted their narrow heads past one another, flailing their slender hooves, or galloping with that easy, floating motion that means every muscle is relaxed. Sometimes the wraith-like visions were blotted out as tears squeezed from between the tightly closed lids of Joey's eyes.

Jim, lying on the other bunk, could not sleep himself; he was conscious of Joey's wakefulness and of his heavy heart. When the knowledge that the little boy was alone with his misery became unbearable, Jim rose and lit the fire and made tea. Then he sat on the edge of Joey's bunk and tried to talk to him of other things. After a while he thought Joey seemed more at ease and he was desperately tired himself after a heavy day, so he went quietly back to his own bunk, turned out the soft light of the kerosene lamp, lay down and fell into a heavy sleep. When he woke it was not much past seven but Joey's bunk was empty.

Joey had risen early and done all the chores. The milk was in the can ready to be carried to Mrs Brett later on. With every second of the time it had taken him to milk the cows and to feed Flash and Trixie, his misery rose. His heart beat faster, then his anxiety swamped him like some great tidal wave – he had to know what was happening, to see the brumby runners and what they were doing to his herd. With his face set in a grim, childish likeness of his father's face, Joey put the bridle on Flash, jumped on his back and turned towards the mountain.

Jim raised himself on an elbow and wondered what to do when he saw Joey's empty bunk. He rose and went outside and found the work all done and Flash gone. He knew that Joey would be on his way to his look-out, to the place from which he had so often watched his precious horses. Jim decided to follow him. At least he would be with the boy if the worst thing of all happened and Joey saw the men take Brumby. He knew he must hurry, the men would time their run to coincide with the morning heat of the sun that would make the brumbies drowsy and off their guard.

Joey turned his head where he lay on his stomach and looked down over the natural corral to the river flats below. When he say his father he managed to give a crooked smile of welcome. He knew why his father had followed him and he was glad, glad that he wanted to be with him in the unhappiness he had tried so hard to bear like a man. It was not really his father's fault, he knew that. Jim hated Dugan and the whole brumby run as much as he did himself.

Jim noticed with pride that Joey had tethered Flash in the shade of a rock; at least his unhappiness had not killed the bushman in Joey. He tied Trixie nearby, and both horses were restless at not being left to graze with the reins over their heads in the usual way. Joey had known as well as Jim did that the sound of the men's shouts, the frightened neighing of the horses, and the crack of stockwhips and the pounding of hooves might prove too startling even for such old-stagers as the ancient Flash and the stolid Trixie.

Climbing the heap of rocks, Jim joined his son. Even before his eyes took in the resting herd, he heard the galloping hooves of the four men's horses. The whip-cracking and shouting had not yet begun, that would come later. Now the men wanted to surprise the resting brumbies and to cut off their exit from the corral. But, bushmen though the brumby runners were, they had reckoned without the alertness and quick reaction, the discipline of the splendid herd.

Yarraman stood in the centre of the grassy space and the other horses moved contentedly around him, pluck-ing an occasional mouthful of grass, quietly settling themselves down after their night at pasture and their run back again, relaxing to doze through the hot, sunlit midday hours. Joey, who knew every wild horse individually, also recognized the two newcomers, Bob Johns's bay mares, where they grazed near to Yarraman.

Before it seemed possible that the first shout could have reached Yarraman's big, hairy, ever-moving ears, he raised his head, reared a little and gave his warning, whistling call. Instantly the discipline he imposed on his herd showed itself. All the horses converged around him while he began his wheeling trot to drive them before him.

The shouts reached all the horses, then the thunderous cracking of whips made them twitch their hides and fling up their heads. Brumby trotted to his mother's side; one of Yarraman's own black colts took the lead, and before the men could reach the gap that led into the corral the horses came pouring through it while Yarra-man wheeled and whistled, nipped and squealed as he bustled the rumps of the laggards.

Joey tried to keep his eyes on Brumby; one of the white backs he looked down on must belong to him. His three pets were somewhere in that stream, Myall and Moonlight and Brumby. His heart pounded and he longed to yell to the horses to hurry, to cheer them on and to shout furiously at the men who had come to harry them. Jim was almost as excited as his son.

'There, Joey!' he shouted. 'There's a herd-leader for you! Your Yarraman'll beat the men yet!'

Joey glowed with pride at the words 'his' Yarraman, and hope touched him fleetingly as he saw the ineffectual effort of the first rider, one of the Campbell boys, to turn the herd back into the corral. His long whip cracked over their straining backs and his shouts were drowned in the rushing sound of their hooves.

Yarraman was behind the horses, urging them on with his whistling neighs, and he came out of the corral last to face the barrage of the four men with their cruel, snaking whips. He never faltered in his stride, not even when a lash caught him across his heavy nose; he only threw his head high and galloped on, his legs moving like pistons, his hairy body streaked with weals wherever the whip-lashes fell.

'He's done it! He's done it!' Jim yelled his excitement as the herd poured down the mountainside, swift and sure-footed, unhampered by riders. The four men came last and the watchers could see that Al Dugan was being left behind on his overworked horse; he drove his spurs into its bleeding sides and cursed at it.

Joey's eyes strained to pick out Brumby as the closely moving herd reached the level land and widened out a little without slowing up, for Yarraman, powerful and determined, thundered at their heels. Joey held his breath as the leading horses reached the first of the treacherous cracks in the dry ground, but they sailed over it until the tail of the herd reached it. Then a brown mare faltered, her hind legs slipped as she tried to jump across edges crumbled by the pounding hooves of the herd, and she fell, scrambling her legs. Yarraman thundered to a stop, whickering and snorting, nudging and pushing her to her feet.

'My word, the old boy's game!' Jim said admiringly. 'They can't bluff him!'

Joey's heart swelled with pride, but his anxious eyes followed the galloping herd, picking out the gleaming white backs from the rushing flood of dark ones. Limping a little, the mare galloped on, but her fall allowed the three leading men, the Campbells and Johns, to come almost level with her. They were after bigger game. Johns wanted his own mares, and with this delay they saw the chance of separating the leader from the rest of the herd. They drove their horses onwards.

The pounding hooves raised the dust into a rolling cloud that sifted downwards until it hung in a misty haze over Yarraman and the mare as Dugan came up behind the stallion. With a shrill challenging scream Yarraman turned to face this new attacker, to block him so that the mare might get away. Dugan's frightened, bony horse, faced with the powerful body, the splayed hooves and the blazing eyes of the brumby stallion, propped and tried to turn.

Dugan yelled and drove his spurs into the bleeding sides of his horse, but for once the horse was more frightened of this great savage beast of his own race than he was of the man. He fought the bit, fought the rowelling spurs, and then the boy and the man, watching through a mist of dust turned to golden motes by the sunlight, saw a dreadful thing. Dugan tugged his horse savagely to a standstill, and as Yarraman reared before him whistling his piercing challenge, he lifted his ·44 and shot the leader down.

With the crack and the whine of the gun Jim heard Joey's cry and he caught the boy and pulled his head against him to shut out the sight, but he could not look away himself. The stallion seemed to rise higher and higher like some towering black cloud, seemed to be forcing his immense body, his striking hooves forward to bring them down on his killer. His hooves thrashed before his erect body silhouetted against the blue sky, then he tottered backwards and crashed to the earth, a fallen monarch of a horse, still struggling, still trying to reach this monster who had doomed him to die so uselessly.

Without another look to be certain that the stallion would not linger on in his agony, Dugan turned his horse and rode on. Jim cursed under his breath and said,

'Don't look, Joey, it won't do any good – in a minute nothing will ever trouble Yarraman again. Wait –'

The dying horse moved feebly, lifted his proud, ugly head and the ghost of his former challenging cry rang out as slowly, slowly his head fell to the ground, his body shuddered and he lay still.

'It's all right now, son.' Jim looked down into Joey's stricken eyes as the little boy whispered,

'He didn't have to do that – he didn't *have* to do it –'

Jim and Joey saw the last of the herd disappear into the trees bordering the creek. The three men were still some way behind them and Dugan toiled along in their wake. The man and the boy gazed into the distance, trying not to see the fallen warrior with the golden dust settling about him. Already overhead floated a dark winged shape whose high, whistling cry proclaimed it a kite. The cawing of the crows, eternal scavengers of the bush, broke discordantly across the warm hush of the morning.

'Joey, we'll take wood out to Yarraman and burn his body. I don't want to leave him for the crows and the dingoes.'

'It doesn't matter to him now,' Joey said dully.

Far off among the trees rose a new jumble of shouting and whip-cracking. Dugan rode into the trees. Out of them, behind him, rushed a terror-stricken white filly.

'Moonlight!' Joey's voice broke. 'Oh, not Moonlight!'

The filly was galloping now towards the mountain, coming closer, her silver-white body darkened to grey by her sweat, her nostrils flaring as the agony of her lungs forced her to draw in more air; one eye was suffused with blood where her desperate straining for speed had ruptured a blood-vessel. She was blind with terror, her only thought was to drive her exhausted legs onwards. Behind her came Dugan's horse with its rider shouting and cursing as he drove his weary horse on to bring him close enough to rope the exhausted, terrified filly.

Joey clutched his father's arm as he saw Dugan, the reins in one hand, the rope ready for the throw in the other. Still Moonlight kept ahead, her fear driving her far past the limit of her normal endurance.

Then it happened. Her head was high as though she was reaching towards the sky for more and purer air. Her sight was dim and her pounding heart rocked her moving body. Her hooves, usually so sure for a yearling, blundered at the rim of one of the earthy cracks and she was down, sprawling across it, kicking feebly, pulling herself out. Dugan had the rope round her neck and the fetlock of one leg was caught in the noose. It tightened round her throat while she wheezed her agony and her bloodshot eyes stared from her head.

Dugan jumped from his horse and it dropped its head in exhaustion while its thin ribs pumped like a bellows. The man pulled the reins over its head and dropped them. Then he walked towards Moonlight, the rope held in one hand, the stockwhip in the other; his face was full of a brutal triumph.

The mare struggled away from him, still on her side, thrashing her slender legs. He slackened the rope a little, giving her a chance to rise, but she only lay on the ground and struggled futilely. His face grew uglier and he brought the lash of the whip savagely across her flank. The beautiful white filly screamed in terror, and Joey, hearing her, put his hands over his ears and his face was as tortured as if the lash had fallen across his own thin body.

Dugan looked down at the struggling filly and his brutal face grew red with fury. He tore the noose from her throat, and from high on the mountain the man and the boy saw him bring the handle of his stockwhip down again and again on the young mare's delicately beautiful head. It was too much for Jim. All sense of the distance between them left him as he sprang to his feet and said in a cold, tight voice,

'I'll kill 'im for that!'

He saw Dugan aim a kick at the filly, then turn away and limp back to his horse, mount it and, kicking it furiously, drive it back towards the trees.

'What's he done to Moonlight?' Joey's childish voice was full of an unbearable pain.

'I don't know. Joey, we can't leave her there.'

'Let me come.'

Jim hesitated, then he said,

'The crows are beginning to move in, I want to get to her as quickly as I can. Can you go home and bring me my gun? Don't carry it loaded, bring the bullets in your pocket – and bring a couple of the long rawhide ropes. Now hurry, remember we've got to do what's best for Moonlight.'

Joey, his heart thumping, his mind sick with apprehension, scrambled down from his rocky perch and went to Flash. Even in the turmoil of his thoughts he remembered to approach Flash slowly. In spite of the loving care Joey had given his horse, any sudden movements towards him brought the reflex action of pure panic. Too often in the past, before Geoff Brett bought Flash and disgustedly found the horse too nervous and too prematurely old for hard work, the sudden pounding of human feet had meant to Flash a cruel tearing at his mouth, the landing of a heavy weight on his weak back, the plunging of spurs into his thin sides. Joey sensed something of this, and whatever his own need for hurry he always went quietly up to Flash and rubbed his head before mounting him.

They set off for home as fast as Joey could persuade Flash to move, and when he looked back as they began their descent of the mountain, he was comforted to see that his father was already out of sight on the far side, out of sight and on his way to help Moonlight.

Flash responded magnificently to Joey's urging. Joey gave him a few mouthfuls of water, not too much, as he tied him in the shade and rushed into the hut. His father's gun leaned in one corner and Joey picked it up with fumbling, anxious hands. He looked in the breech as he had always been told to do. It was empty. He found the ammunition box and took what he had been told to take. His father's rawhide ropes hung coiled from a nail; Joey climbed on the rough wooden chair and lifted two of them down. Then with the ropes coiled round one shoulder and the gun dragging the other shoulder down, he went back to Flash.

Flash didn't care for guns; hidden in them were memories of merciless chases through rough bush that tore and whipped at his sides, of the cruel pounding on his ribs until exhaustion dulled pain and left him with only a sickening terror and a body too tired to react to it. After the gun was fired came the frightening smell of blood, and the skin of some slaughtered animal was added to his already over-heavy load.

It took Joey five minutes to reassure Flash that he could be trusted not to repeat any of the horrors of the past because he carried a gun, five minutes in which he kept his anxiety and impatience within bounds. Then they were on their way, and the weight of the gun made Joey's right arm ache fiercely.

At the best speed they could manage it was nearly an hour before Joey and Flash drew near to Moonlight. The filly still lay on her side. Sometimes her legs thrashed feebly as she lifted her pathetically battered young head and made abortive attempts to rise. Squatting in the blazing heat and dust of the plain, Jim was far enough away not to worry the mare, yet near enough to circle quietly about her as he kept the crows away and tried to find out what had happened to her that she could not rise. One thing he knew, her legs were unbroken. He walked to meet Joey.

'I won't need the gun. She's either damaged her spine or slipped a muscle, either way we might be able to get 'er better.'

He looked at Joey's tired face, streaked with sweat and grime, and they smiled at each other as the little boy rubbed his numbed right arm.

'We've got to get 'er home somehow,' Jim went on. 'Whatever we do she'll be frightened, so I'll have to tie her legs and blindfold 'er.'

Great black clouds of small flies zoomed about, sometimes settling on the filly, and Joey watched them anxiously. He knew that animals, even more than humans, got sandy blight from these flies, and that it often brought blindness to the bush creatures. The horrible little flies were attracted by the blood and broken, swollen flesh around one of Moonlight's eyes, the one on which Dugan's blows had landed. A moment's inattention and the injured eye was covered in a mass of flies like a black patch. There was not much that could be done to keep them off. As fast as Jim brushed them away they settled again, and any movement near to the filly terrified her. Jim swung himself on to Trixie's broad back.

'Come on, we'll see if we can find enough broken boughs to make a kind of litter for Moonlight. Pity I haven't an axe. You couldn't have carried it as well as the rifle and – well, I thought we might have needed the rifle more than the axe.'

'I'm glad we don't,' Joey said almost joyfully, then his face clouded over. He said passionately, 'I'd like to kill that Dugan!'

They rode into the scrub, leaving the mare. Out of the tangle of storm-felled branches, by using the rawhide ropes, Jim made a kind of raft. Then he found four stout sticks and he and the boy went back to the filly with Trixie dragging the strange arrangement behind her.

'It's going to frighten the poor little beggar when we put this over her, but we'll have to do it, this heat's too hard on her. Then I'll go and get Geoff, we'll need help. Listen!'

They stood still and heard the sound of shouts and of horses crashing through the undergrowth. Then the Campbell boys came into the open followed by Bob Johns, and after him came Dugan, still driving his exhausted horse.

With Bob Johns leading one, and Frank Campbell the other, came Johns's two bay mares. The mares had not been long enough among the wild horses to acquire their stamina or cunning at evading capture, and they were caught after a hard chase.

Joey's heart beat with joy; they had not caught

Brumby or Myall or any of the horses he loved. He didn't care about the two mares, they were used to being handled. Dugan was empty-handed.

Jim hailed the riders and walked to meet them leading Trixie, leaving the strange litter on the ground.

'What kind of a contraption is that?' Bob Johns asked.

'Joey and I are goin' to try and get the filly back home, she might get all right, I don't think she's got any broken bones.' He ignored Dugan. Frank Campbell handed the lead to Johns and he and his brother swung down from their horses.

'Here, we'll give you a hand. She's a bit much for you two on your own.'

Joey swelled with pride at being casually counted as a man.

'Thanks,' Jim said. 'I was just goin' for help, save a lot of time if you don't mind.'

'Glad to. I didn't see 'er fall when we were runnin' the brumbies – an' what on earth happened to her head?'

Dugan pushed forward. He was in a foul humour and as usual he blamed his horse. He had organized the run, and the only one who had got anything out of it was Bob Johns. Still in the saddle, his angry eyes looked down at Jim and he hunched his heavy shoulders. Jim looked steadily back at him without speaking. Dugan said,

'That filly's mine! She's no use an' I'm gonna shoot 'er.'

Jim spoke, 'You had your chance to get the filly – an' what's more you've done your share of shootin' today.'

Dugan's face was suffused with temper, and he jumped off his horse, glaring at Jim.

'Th' filly's mine an' I'm shootin' 'er here an' now!'

Joey, watching with horrified eyes, was conscious of the three men who stood quietly by, making no move to interfere. Then he fixed his eyes on his father who was facing Dugan. He heard the cold, sliding click of the breechlock, and then his father moved too quickly for his eyes to follow. The next thing he saw was Dugan's gun falling from his hands while Dugan himself seemed jerked backwards, his knees buckled, and he fell and lay still in the dust. Jim stepped back and ran the palm of his left hand over the bleeding knuckles of his right.

'Knocked 'im cold!' Bob Johns's voice was full of satisfaction. None of them liked Dugan and his brutal shooting of Yarraman had disgusted them.

'Mess up your hand much, Jim?' one of the Campbells asked.

'Worth it,' Jim answered briefly. Then he turned and smiled at the awed Joey, whose gentle nature had been so outraged by the man on the ground that he could only look at his father's handiwork with profound satisfaction. Jim stepped over the prone body and took the long rope from Joey, calling to the Campbells,

'If you'll hitch this contraption of mine on to Trixie – Joey'll hold 'er – I'll rope the filly an' we'll roll 'er on to it.'

Joey ran to Trixie's head and stood stroking her broad velvet nose while the Campbells went to work. Jim roped the frightened filly's legs together as gently as he could. He hesitated a minute, thinking the damage to the filly's eye had already been done, but then he tore the rolled-up sleeve off his own shirt and bandaged her eyes with it, knowing that the journey would be less terrifying for her if she couldn't see at all.

No one took the slightest notice of Dugan who had begun to revive by rolling on to his face and then coming to rapidly as he coughed and spat away the dust. He also spat out the broken halves of two teeth. By the time the three men had the filly on the litter Dugan was glaring round him, pulling his slow wits together. Finally he got to his feet and shouted,

'I'll get you for this, Meehan — you an' the filly, an' that kid of yours, too!'

'Oh, dry up!' Jim began good-naturedly. As far as he was concerned the affair was over and he hoped he would never see Dugan again. Then the implied threat to Joey registered and he stopped what he was doing and stood upright, six feet of leathery, work-hardened bushman, and he looked steadily across the glittering air at the other man.

'Dugan, if you ever touch my kid, I'll belt you so's you won't come round for a week. You remember that, because I mean it!'

Joey was thrilled by his father's defence of himself. He felt he should back him up, remind him that he, Joey, was really a man and could look after himself.

'An' if he ever touches Moonlight I'll kill him myself!' he shouted, drunk with his father's power.

The men, all except Dugan, roared with laughter, but Joey didn't mind. He and his father were the sort of men who could take a joke, he told himself, and as he looked down at his short brown legs, his skinny little body, he grinned himself; he supposed it did sound kinda funny! Only Dugan saw no joke in it.

'Why, you —' he began, and Jim took a step towards him. Hunching his shoulders, Dugan limped heavily towards his tired horse, mounted, and without a word to anyone, rode off. 'Good riddance,' muttered one of the Campbells, and the other silently agreed with him.

'Funny bloke,' said Bob Johns, sitting sideways in his saddle and gazing after the departing Dugan. 'Look at the way he's beltin' 'is horse! They say it was a horse that twisted his back and gave him that limp an' that 'e's hated all horses ever since.'

Jim straightened up from blindfolding Moonlight and looked up at the sky.

'Goin' to storm later on,' he remarked briefly and the others agreed. Dark clouds like dense, rolling smoke were pushing up from the horizon into the clear sky, and the wind brought the ghostly rumble of far-off thunder. When everything was ready for moving Moonlight, Jim called to Johns.

'Glad you got your mares back, Bob, but keep 'em this time. I'm havin' no more brumby runs over my land, no matter whose stock's missin' – O.K.?'

'O.K., Jim. Well, I can't help so I think I'll push off with my mares. Sorry you boys didn't have any luck!'

'We had some pretty good fun,' Tom Campbell said. 'But, my word, I'd 'a liked that colt I chased for a while.'

'Which one?' Joey asked.

'One of two silver-white colts, a really tough boy – and fast! Dunno how we missed 'im.'

'That was Brumby,' Joey said proudly. The others laughed.

'Got 'em all named, have you?'

Jim joined in, 'If you fellers haven't chased 'em off for good, those brumbies 're goin' to be Joey's herd. That's why we're havin' no more brumby-runnin' over our land, eh, Joey?'

'You bet we aren't!' Joey answered promptly. Even though his beloved herd was scattered, right then his heart was singing, because though splendid Yarraman had been killed, all the others were safe – somewhere. If he could only tell them how safe they'd be if they would come back again! Moonlight, little Moonlight was his and he'd make her better, he'd look after her so well and love her so much that she *must* get better. Joey's spirits soared so that he hardly noticed his tired body.

Then they began dragging Moonlight towards home.

The filly was so near exhaustion that her fear-reactions were numbed. She was afraid and in pain, but somehow it all seemed far away and she didn't struggle. Although the journey was by no means smooth, she had no broken bones from which to suffer agony at every bump. Jim borrowed Tom Campbell's horse and rode on ahead, leaving him to ride Trixie, and Joey managed to make Flash keep up with his father, so there would be no waiting for the invalid.

It was latish when they reached the hut. Joey and his father had fixed a place in the stable for Moonlight. They used a lavish amount of bedding and when Trixie finally began the last climb up the slope, with Tom Campbell riding her and the strange litter dragging behind her heels, everything was ready.

When Moonlight had been bedded down and the Campbells had ridden off to the accompaniment of the two Meehans' grateful thanks, Jim and Joey settled down to do what they could for Moonlight. So much had happened to the silver filly that she lay almost passively while Jim bathed her eye with the boracic-doctored water that Joey brought him.

'How is it, Dad? Is it very bad?' Joey asked.

'Pretty bad,' Jim answered. 'The flies had a good go at it. But even if she loses the sight of one eye the other one seems all right. Now all we can do is to try and get her to trust us, to tame her, and it won't be easy. It might be hard to feed and water her too, but I know you've got plenty of patience. Then if, as I think, she only has a slipped muscle, she might get all right. Perhaps she'll never be any good to ride, but if she does get better then in a few years, Joey, you'll have your first brood mare – how'll you like that?'

Joey beamed. 'Will she be all right if I go to school tomorrow and leave her? I'd like to tell Mrs Brett!'

'Yes, she's better alone. In a couple of days we'll try and get her on her feet. It's no good for horses to lie down all the time. Come on now, it'll storm later, then we'll come back to the filly again.'

Joey put his hand firmly on Moonlight's shoulder, the way it wouldn't frighten her, and with his forefinger he furrowed the silver hair. In the parting the filly's skin showed black – Arabian black; Joey looked up at his father and smiled.

They walked out into air darkened by the approaching storm, while far-off lightning split the purple clouds in forked, quivering lines of white fire.

Part Two: The Captive

The terrified brumbies poured through the bush, running wild without Yarraman's leadership, their one idea escape from the shouting men and the thunderous cracks of the whips. Brumby ran beside his mother. He was frightened, gripped by the panic that drove the rest of the herd, yet comforted by the occasional touch of the bay mare's swollen, sweat-streaked side as he raced beside her.

Suddenly, right on the heels of the galloping herd which so far had kept in fairly close formation, came the shouting of men's voices and a terrifying volley of sound from their stockwhips. That completed the demoralization of the herd. Without a leader to take charge each horse thought only of itself, blundering and crashing, whinnying and whistling, propping and wheeling, or merely galloping onwards in a frenzy of fear.

Brumby felt his mother wheel and followed her just as two men with swinging ropes rode into the herd and went straight for the other bay mares, the newcomers. The rest of the herd, manes and tails flying, eyes wild, plunged through the bush, leaped fallen logs, crashed through scrub, running wildly anywhere in their efforts to escape the pursuing men. With lungs bursting and hearts thudding their strong legs carried them onwards and they did escape the men, but Brumby's mother knew that she could not keep up with the herd, burdened as she was by her soon-to-be-born foal. She turned at right angles to the rushing horses, pushing Brumby with her side, giving the tremulous whinny that a mare gives her foal in times of danger. They went through the thick scrub, their hides clutched by thorny bushes and torn by the jagged ends of dry, broken sticks, and they escaped.

Gradually the sounds died out behind them and the mare dropped to a trot and took more care about nosing the way around obstacles instead of rushing through them. Both mare and yearling were caked with sweat. The moisture which had sprung from their bodies became a dry coating as the hot air absorbed the liquid and left the salt. The darkness of the sweat-streaks faded on the bay mare and a white scum took their place, but on Brumby's pale hide the salt was not noticeable.

Soon mother and son dropped to a walk, instinctively nearing the water which they so badly needed. Their breathing quietened down, but their eyes still rolled and they both started nervously at the slightest movement from the bush around them; a twig disturbed by bird or beast, or the rustle of leaves in the fitful breeze.

On and on they went. Perhaps the mare knew that night would bring new life to her and she wanted to be far from her enemies. After they had covered some ten miles of the rough country they came to a small creek. When the breeze blew the brave scent of water to Brumby's nostrils he broke into a trot. The mare followed more slowly, but in a few minutes both horses were muzzle-deep in the water, drinking in big, silent gulps that, as their need became fulfilled, changed to a capricious sucking at the surface of the water. They made bird-like noises interspersed with stamping in the shallows where the coolness felt delicious on hooves and fetlocks, and the sharp blows of their hooves sent showers of cool crystal drops over their sweat-caked shoulders and backs.

Refreshed, they pushed their way through the tangle that edged the water and came out on to the clearer ground beyond. They made for a clump of ironbarks that would have provided needed shade if the sullen clouds had not already done so.

After the long journey, much of it at a swift, driven pace, and with the terror of being hunted, the mare and the yearling stood resting quietly beneath the trees, shaking their heads and switching their tails to keep away the swarms of flies that tormented them.

Around them the light gradually took on an ominous greenish hue, but they were lost in their need for sleep; storms were nothing new even in the yearling's brief life. They opened their eyes and shifted their hooves uneasily when the first low rolling of thunder reached them. As it came nearer and cracked sharply above them, Brumby threw up his head and gave a small squeal of fright; the sound reminded him of the menace of the men with their stockwhips, and he moved nearer to his mother. When she showed no fear he went away again, disturbed and hungry, and put his muzzle near the ground as he searched for grass roots.

The storm rolled overhead and heavy gusts of wind sent the horses' tails fluttering against their hocks and blew their ragged manes and forelocks forward as they turned their rumps to the fury of the storm. A slanting squall of rain struck them and dissolved the stale salt of their exertions, washing it from their hides.

Like quivering nerves the lightning played about the clouds and the storm rolled majestically overhead. The crash of thunder and the flash of lightning almost synchronized. The mare stood quietly, partly sheltered by the trees, unmoved by wind or rain, but Brumby, his unmatured nervous system still on edge, trotted about, giving little whinnies of fright at the flashes of blinding light, the sudden noisy crashes that hurt his sensitive ears.

The louring clouds above them seemed to press down on the lightning. At the edge of the mass of purple clouds, torn scraps of fleecy grey raced about, driven by the wind that was as yet unable to move or thin out the heavy, thunder-filled mass of the storm clouds, but merely able to tear great shreds from them to make vaporous forms, thinning, twisting and moving, racing across the sky like hunted wild things, as the brumby herd had raced across the earth below them earlier in the day.

Then Brumby, who had trotted just beyond the clump of trees and wheeled to join his mother again, was blinded by a ghastly brilliance of unnatural light, which was followed by a rending crash. The sound seemed to tear at his flesh. He reared, squealing his fear. In an instant the unbearable brilliance had gone, the thunder rolled menacingly away and the air was filled with a fiery, metallic smell.

The colt turned towards where his mother had been standing. She was no longer upright but had fallen in a tumbled mass. Beside her the lightning had torn the big ironbark in half; the leafy end of the tree lay away from the mare while the torn, jagged stump rose above where she lay. It was blackened and smouldering and the ground all around was seared and dark too.

The mare was dead, but Brumby, who had never seen death, and who knew nothing of the real terror of lightning but only of its flash and the sound of the following thunder, went hesitantly towards the still body, shaking his head and snorting the bitter, acrid smell from his nostrils.

He stepped delicately beside her and whickered. There was no soft, answering sound. The burnt smell of the grass and the smell from where her hide had been smitten and scorched by the lightning frightened him. He stood uncertainly, twisting his neck and turning back his top lip. Then he went closer and put his head down and sniffed at the mare wonderingly. Was this his mother? It had none of the good, reassuring smell of clean hide. He whinnied piteously, all at once he felt the full weight of his loneliness. The lightning still flickered in the sky, but the storm was passing into the far-off roll and rumble of thunder.

All that night Brumby stood beside his mother, sometimes whickering at her, touching her with his soft muzzle and then pulling his head back from the strange, unpleasant smell that lingered about her body; sometimes he pawed gently at her as a dog might have done.

There had been no problem of birth for the mare, there was no problem about anything at all any more. All about Brumby was a terrible solitude.

Thirst grew in him. At dawn he picked his way hesitantly to the creek. As he bent his head to drink he jerked it back again and looked wildly at the far bank. A thin, half-grown dingo pup stood at the water's edge looking across at the foal with his slanting golden eyes. The foal jerked back, but the dingo was not afraid and went quietly on with the business of lapping up the water. Brumby stood looking at it doubtfully.

Except that he had never seen a wild dog before, he felt no fear, only a certain wariness. He had never known what it was to be harried by any dog. Since the other animal was drinking he put his head down and drank himself. The watery rings from where the dingo lapped and from where the horse ruffled the water drawing it in through his teeth rippled outwards and converged, distorting the images of the wide golden face and the narrow, intelligent white head.

When the dingo finished drinking it slipped back into the undergrowth. Brumby drew back from the water and went slowly and unwillingly back to where lay the thing that had once been his warm, breathing mother.

He lingered near to the mare's body because he did not know what else to do. He, who had spent all his short life with his kind, in a community of horses dominated by the stallion and composed of the comforting forms of twenty or more wild horses, was now completely lost without direction or companionship.

Each day he went to the creek several times, and his hunger sent him circling around looking for grass. But he never went out of sight of the clump of trees and what lay under them. At least twice a day the dingo pup came down to drink when Brumby was there. After the first day he ceased to think it strange, and rather welcomed seeing another living creature.

When the crows descended on the body of his mother, Brumby returned from the bank of the creek to find a raucous, flapping, screeching mass of big blue-black birds scurrying across his mother's body, cawing loudly, flapping their wings as they balanced on her swollen form, and something of fear and outrage touched the colt's wild mind so that he charged at them again and again.

The crows' feathers were purple-black in the sunlight as a dozen birds rose screeching, while fifty more went on with their horrible feasting. Again and again Brumby charged, shaking his head and stamping his hooves at the birds until, discouraged, he moved away a little and stood, solitary and bewildered, watching with frightened eyes the business of disintegration that was happening to all that was left of the warm comfort, the companion-ship and protection that had been his mother.

In a dispirited way he left the big birds to their scavenging and searched for grass himself, but he never went far away.

On the third day the bones began to show their stark whiteness from the torn bay hide, and the foetid smell, the hundreds of screaming, pecking birds, made him realize at last that it was no use waiting and hoping for the warm hide, the gentle nickerings and nudgings, and the feeling of security and love to return to him. He was alone.

That night he crossed the creek and stayed in the shelter of the thick scrub on the other side. At dawn he went to the creek. The hindquarters and drooping tail of the dingo were before him and he went slowly to the water and drank beside the wild dog.

Then the morning breeze brought the frightening smell of death, of stale, rotting flesh and corruption, and he threw up his head and wheeled, turning back into the scrub, moving farther and farther into it until the foul breeze ceased to pursue him.

Now that he had broken away from all that bound him, the memories and securities of the small foal he had been, he moved on into a world that was strange to him, a world of sharp-thorned bushes, an arid land littered with dead logs, and his hunger drove him on to try and find better grazing.

He walked uncertainly across the rough earth, putting his hooves down carefully, starting when a stick cracked, and blowing down his nostrils at every strange sound, sometimes stopping and lifting his head to nicker, send-ing out his call to his kind. Hesitating, walking or break-ing into a jog, he covered several miles, and once he saw the golden-red form of the young dingo slipping through the trees near to him and he whickered as he might have done had he seen another foal. The dingo stopped and lifted his head, and Brumby could see the golden eyes set in the triangular face as he looked at him.

What the colt could not know was that the young dingo was as lonely as himself. Traps and guns had killed all his family two days before Brumby had first seen him. He too missed the security of the dark lair in which he had been born, the silently moving forms of his parents and the fun of his games with his brother and sister. These had been silent games, in which they played at catching living things that would in time become their food. In this natural way all their hunting muscles, their eyesight, and their self-protective instincts would be fully developed when the time came for the parent dogs to force them out into a life of their own. From the entrance to the lair, when that time came, they would have met with snarls and quick snaps when they tried to enter, so that they would have turned away to begin their adult lives.

The need for independence had not come to this solitary pup through the parent dogs but through the interference of man. Only the one pup had escaped and he still limped from a bullet that had passed through one flank without touching the bone. Fortunately for the pup he was big enough to hunt small game and to keep himself alive, but the early disruption of his family life had the effect of making him long for the company of some living thing, anything young and wild, even if not of his own kind.

As the days went on Brumby journeyed through the scrub until eventually it gave on to grassland. The young dingo paralleled his wanderings; gradually the two learned to travel together and to get some comfort from each other's living presence.

The Brumby

When the silver yearling slept through the hushed, hot noonday, the dingo lay near by, instinct sending him to lie with his hindquarters against rock or tree or earthy bank, any solid substance that would prevent an enemy's surprise attack from the rear, and he dozed too. He opened his golden eyes at intervals to watch the light and shade flickering on the silver hide of his companion, to hear the comforting noise of the movement of his hooves as he shifted position and dozed with automatic switchings of his tail and shakings of his head.

In all the vast wilderness about them, Brumby saw none of his kind. No tame horses grazed the untouched land and the brumby herd were scattered and far away. Sometimes other dingoes would slip through the bush near to the yearling and his friend, ghostly creatures, silvered by the moonlight and moving in absolute silence; or the sound of their wails would come through the night air, a mournful howling on the sustained double note that makes the dingoes' cry differ from that of all other canines.

Once a wild dog circled about the place where Brumby and the young dingo were resting. Its broad face appeared between the trees or around bushes as it moved about them. The young dingo lay watching, his eyes open, his body shivering with excitement, until at last he was unable to lie still, and he rose and moved towards where he had seen the other dog.

Had he been a bitch all would have been well, for the older dingo was looking for a mate. But when the young dog faced him, the older one snarled and leapt at the half-grown pup in sudden fury. The pup yelped and tumbled backwards and the hairy body of the other was on him.

Brumby, startled by the sudden noise, sprang nervously to attention. There was nothing silent about the way the half-grown wild dog received the attack. He yelped his fear and pain as a domesticated dog might have done.

Brumby was thoroughly startled. The snarling, yelping, entangled golden forms rolled towards him, and he snorted, whinnied and reared up once or twice before wheeling and dashing into the scrub. The following sounds from the yelping young dingo terrified him; with mane and tail flying he galloped a few yards, stopped, wheeled round and faced the sound, and then nervously went on.

The big male dingo soon tired of punishing the pup for daring to be a male when it was searching for a female. It stopped its attack, stood stiff-legged over the pup's squirming body for a second or two, then disengaged itself and disappeared silently into the bush.

The pup sat up. He was not badly hurt, but his bitten hide stung him and he whimpered softly to himself as he licked his wounds and looked around for his friend. His wounds attended to, his loneliness became absolute. He got to his feet, and ran whimpering from side to side of the little clearing, looking for Brumby, longing for the comfort of a living presence.

Brumby stood very still at the top of a small rise, his head lifted so that his sensitive nostrils were dilated as he tried to catch a hint of his friend on the wind. He too felt lonely and desolate. He moved about restlessly, but there was no spring in his movements. Dingo was the one living thing in a world that was filled with loneliness, the one link with the security of his earlier life, for in an instinctive way Brumby linked the dingo pup with the mother who had been his protector for so long. His need for friendship, for some form of life to companion him, all centred on the wild dog.

The yearling stood with drooping head, dispirited and

lonely; in a small clearing a quarter of a mile away the pup with drooping head and tail was lonely too. He sat back on his haunches and lifted his blunt nose to the sky and gave his immature, sorrowful wail. Again the unsure wailing cry carried through the still air.

Brumby's ears shot forward; he turned his lifted head this way and that way as he sniffed the breeze, then walked towards the sound. He came hesitantly out of the bush into the small clearing as the pup was filling his chest for another mournful cry. He heard the sound of hooves and sat listening. Brumby stepped into the clearing and the dingo ran to him; when Brumby put his soft muzzle down and blew through his nostrils, Dingo licked his nose. Brumby jerked his head back, then he must have decided there was something friendly about that warm tongue, for he poked his head forward again, snorting nervously as he caught the scent of blood from Dingo's bitten hide.

They settled down comfortably for the night, their loneliness forgotten; in the morning they wandered on their way again.

After Moonlight had been in the stable for two or three days, Jim said they must try to get her on her feet. The filly was no longer terrified when they came near to her. Both of them, but Joey particularly, had spent many hours petting and talking to her, bathing her eyes and otherwise ministering to her comfort. She was not friendly, but neither was she afraid. Her eye was still in a shocking condition and here and there her head was marked and swollen where the hard handle of Dugan's stockwhip had struck it.

'We can't save the sight of that eye,' Jim said, shaking his head as he looked at the silver filly.

'Will it heal up?'

'Yes, I think it'll heal. But it's been so badly damaged, and the flies didn't help.'

'Poor little Moonlight! Anyway, I don't care, I'll love her just as much if she only has one eye and if she never walks,' Joey said stoutly.

Jim smiled. 'I know you will. You've got to make up your mind that she'll never be fit to ride, but she may become a first-class brood mare and that's what you want, isn't it?'

Joey nodded and his father went on,

'We'll give her some sun and air when the eye heals a bit.'

Joey looked around the dim stable. They deliberately kept the filly in the dark because of her injured eye, and because the vicious clouds of bush-flies do not enter buildings; the larger house-flies are not such virulent carriers of eye disease.

Moonlight lay on her dry bedding, her slim silvery body shining against the pale gold of the straw she lay on. Feeding was a problem, but she drank plenty of water and her battered eye needed the shelter.

After three days Jim and Joey made her get on to her feet. It was evident that the near hind leg would not take any weight. She stood well enough on the other three legs, but when they tried to lead her gently a few steps, she simply fell down again.

With an anxious face Joey wiped his hot hands on his dilapidated shorts and stood silently by while his father struggled with the mare. When she was on her feet again they made no attempt to move her.

'Joey – get some of that special feed Geoff gave you.'

Joey leapt to it. After Moonlight had snorted a little at the bucket in which he had put the feed, she condescended to eat. Jim stood by, lounging against a post and rolling a cigarette. He nodded his head as Joey, his face beaming, held the bucket until Moonlight finished the last mouthful.

'She'll do,' Jim said briefly. 'Now I'll have to get to work. You get Flash and start for school.'

'But Moonlight might fall down.'

'She might, but she'll fall soft on all that straw. There's nothing to worry about. Ask Mrs Brett to let you come back half an hour earlier, if you like.'

Joey's face brightened. He loved school, but he loved Moonlight more than anything in the world except, maybe, Brumby – and, of course, his father. He wondered where Brumby was and thought sadly of him for a moment before he was comforted by the thought of the yearling leading the wild life to which he had been born.

He went for the milkcan, put the bridle on Flash and was on his way after a last quick look at Moonlight where she was still standing in more or less the attitude of a resting horse. She took no notice at all of Joey.

The boy tried very hard to keep his mind on his lessons, but it really was difficult not to worry about Moonlight being alone. Because she had so few real school books from which to teach Joey, Mrs Brett made up her own lessons for him, and interlarded them lavishly with all sorts of stories and any references she could find about horses from her ancient encyclopedia.

Signs of inattention were never punished, Joey was bright and he wanted to learn, and when he was inattentive it was for other reasons he could not control. This usually meant a reward in the form of a special story or something of the sort in which horses figured largely.

Try as he would Joey could not keep from thinking about Moonlight: was she all right? Had she fallen? Mrs Brett sighed. She had begun to teach him something of Greek history by means of simple stories and fables. Now she told him of the Sybarites who taught their horses to dance. This captured Joey's wandering attention and he was delighted with his 'history' lesson when she told him how, when the cunning Crotonians wanted to conquer the Sybarites, they played dance music, and instead of charging into battle, the Sybarites' horses began to dance! Of course the Crotonians won that battle, and Joey was enchanted with the picture of a regiment of dancing horses.

His attention wandered again when this item from the past merged into more solid history. He really tried to listen but in his mind he was watching Moonlight with himself mounted on her back, dancing to Bill Regan's accordion. The Moonlight of his vision had both large dark eyes and four sound legs; he sighed when he was brought back to reality.

Brumby and his dingo friend wandered onwards, always searching for more feed for the young horse. Dingo managed to feed himself on the small life around him. On moonlight nights the wild dog and the wild horse would play their games on the vast plains over which they travelled. These were always chasing games. Dingo crept to where Brumby stood, his head moving up and down, giving loud snorts and pawing the ground. When he advanced to within a few yards of where Brumby stood, Dingo crouched flat against the earth, his belly pressed on to the grass, and he waited alertly until Brumby charged at him. Then he would be away, with the silver horse chasing him, galloping flat out, wheeling, charging, and snorting, the moonlight turning his hide to white fire. Over and over they repeated the pattern of the game until, tired out, they stopped and dozed in their separate manner, but always near to each other.

What neither animal knew was that they, in their wild

state, were repeating a pattern common to domesticated horses and dogs. Many racers and many show horses have refused to race or show themselves at their best unless their favourite cat or dog, companion of their stables, travelled with them.

Sometimes a station dog will become attached to a stockhorse whether or not his master is riding it. When that horse is turned out to grass, perhaps for four or five months at a time, the dog goes with it, living as dingoes live on the wild game about him, prowling or sleeping near the horse of his choice, sometimes playing as Brumby and Dingo played.

In their wanderings they covered a great deal of country, often circling back on their tracks, and both fed well and grew mightily. In six months Brumby was a powerful young horse, his ungroomed coat gleaming with health. His muscles began to bunch beneath his hide and the crest to form under the wild tangle of his mane. But both Brumby and Dingo were still young enough to need the emotional dependence they had cultivated in each other, the need of a living companion in lives that were solitary from their own kind.

When their wanderings took them into cattle country, Brumby looked in amazement at these creatures that were so like, and yet so unlike, himself. At first the roaring of the bulls alarmed him, then it aroused his curiosity.

When the moon shone down on them with a light that was almost as bright as day, he and Dingo finished their game and moved aimlessly onwards. They came to their first fence, a rough post-and-rails affair. Brumby turned and walked curiously along it while Dingo slipped through it and looked back for his friend to follow. Brumby did not know what to make of this barrier. He stopped and pushed his head between the rails. Nothing

moved, so he struck at the lower railing with his strong, unshod hoof. The railing felt very solid.

From the distance came the roaring of a bull, a deep, rumbling ominous sound that one bull uses to another, a mighty male challenge in a voice of low thunder that stockmen mimic with human words, 'I'm a bull! I'm a bull!' then the defiant, high-screaming answer, the bull's counterpart to the human words, 'I know you are! I know you are!'

Brumby lifted his head and listened, his quickly turned ears channelling the night sounds to his brain. A little way farther on the top railing had been forced off by sheer animal strength and it lay where it had fallen on the ground on the other side of the fence. The heavy, restless animal, that had dislodged it as the heat of battle rose within him, forced his way into the paddock from which he could hear the far-off challenge of another bull. Brumby stepped over the lower railing and moved into the paddock, too. He walked towards the noise and Dingo slipped through the grass after him.

As he drew near the noise, the huge red rump of a Hereford bull was before him. The massive beast stood tearing up the earth with its cloven hooves and feinting with its sharp horns. Clods of earth tangled with grass roots rose in the air and fell back on to the red shoulders. The bull bent low to the ground, turning its head from side to side as it pushed its lethal horns in a hooking movement, furrowing the earth's crust as though it were sharpening the horn-tips.

Facing it, twenty yards away, stood another bull of the same breed, an older bull, strong in its maturity and gradually working itself up into an overflow of wrath. It too tore the ground, shook its great head and covered its forequarters in crumbled earth, and sharpened its horns.

Brumby was amazed, he had never seen such a sight

as this. In his youthful ignorance he stood in the most dangerous place possible, directly behind the huge beast which was bellowing forth its challenge. Brumby stamped and propped and tossed his head himself; the noise and movement excited him. He stamped furiously, raised his head and whinnied loudly, but luckily for him the sound was lost in the growling thunder that came from the broad white chests of the two colossi who, if they heard Brumby through their own rumblings, completely ignored him.

Then with a roar that seemed to split the air, the two beasts charged at each other. There was the crash of the solid frontal bones meeting, the lighter, more sinister clashing of horns as they rattled to the twisting of their heads. The bulls dug their hooves into the earth and strained, snorting and grunting, against each other. Neither would disengage its head, the enormous wrinkled necks held muscles that counterbalanced each move to drive past an opponent's head and so hook the horns into fleshy neck or side.

Panting, with streels of saliva dripping from their mouths, the red monsters drew back, tore up the earth and then, bellowing at each other, charged again. Again they locked horns and struggled, and Brumby, head high and nostrils wide, trembled with excitement.

Then the heavier, matured strength of the far bull told. Inch by inch, bunching its muscles and driving its hooves into the earth, the older bull bore down its rival. They struggled silently except for the great gales of breath that were expelled by their efforts, and their deep grunts. Their bellies almost touched the ground, and the younger bull was forced back fighting every inch of the way as its broad rump was pushed towards where the excited Brumby stood. Then the younger bull's strength gave, it turned blindly and blundered away from the older bull's charge. Suddenly the victor found itself relieved of the weight of its opponent against its own curly white forehead, and it went in a straight line, past where the younger bull had struggled, to where Brumby stood so amazed as to be unmoving.

Without intent, wanting only to check its forward rush, the winning bull barged straight into the young horse, knocked him over and blundered on across his body. Brumby squealed in terror and tried to rise. The bull's weight had knocked the breath out of him, but somehow he got to his feet, trembling with fear, to see the lumbering giant turning now and making for him again, this time with intent.

Brumby did not wait. He was filled with fear of this powerful, fleshy red engine before him, and he turned and raced for the fence. In his excitement he remembered nothing about the broken rail through which he had entered the paddock, he thought of nothing but getting away from that ton of flesh that was bearing down on him.

Although the wild horse often jumped fallen logs during his games with Dingo, he had never been faced with anything higher nor anything that he was not in the mood to jump. Now the fence loomed before him, solid in the moonlight, while behind him he heard the snorting rumbling of the now thoroughly aroused bull, and the thunderous impact of its hooves growing nearer.

He dashed at the fence, rose like a bird on the wings of his fear, was over it and galloping across the paddock. He went across the corner of the paddock diagonally and another fence rose before him. He could no longer hear the bull through the wild beating of his heart for his terror was still with him. Easily and with beautiful grace his strong white body rose and cleared the railings.

Once across the second fence, Brumby dropped to a

walk, nostrils dilated, ribs pumping like bellows. He stood a moment, looking fearfully backwards. Then his glance fell on Dingo, standing near him, red tongue out, sides heaving like his own, and the sight reassured him. He lowered his head and Dingo came forward formally and licked his nose. Brumby gave a little snort of relief. His breath came back; he was in magnificent condition and would not feel his bruises for several hours, and not very much then considering the avalanche of flesh and muscle and bone that had charged over him.

Moving quietly now Brumby and his wild friend disappeared into the familiar scrub, walking mile after tangled mile, unwilling to rest until they were well away from the scene of their terrifying experience.

Once, in the worst heat of the summer, when the grass was sparse and brown and Brumby thin and hungry, washed by the hot yellow sunlight that burned away the leaves that might have provided shade, he had his first experience of the flaming red devils that raged in bush-fires.

All Brumby knew at first was that the air was smoky and hotter than even the sun made it, and that Dingo, whose instincts had a longer history and were more alive to the dangers of his own land than were Brumby's, began running back and forward just in front of him, and then circling round behind him to urge him onwards.

Dingo's ancestors had lived in this ancient land of theirs for millions of years before Brumby's immediate relations had become the first horses on Australian soil, and the wild dog knew instinctively what fire meant in terms of danger. Brumby objected to the smell and the taste of the air and flung his head about disgustedly, curling his upper lip back from the square ivory pegs of his teeth and dilating his nostrils in his efforts to dispel the unaccustomed smell. He looked in amazement at the

variety of creatures that raced by him, wallabies, bandi-
coots, goannas, snakes, they and their smaller creeping
brethren; large centipedes, big spiders and innumerable
beetles, mice and lizards streamed through the dry grass,
none of them taking the slightest notice of the others.
Deadly enemies ran side by side and never glanced at
each other.

At last all the strangeness around him, the agitation of
Dingo, began to worry Brumby. Something was expected
of him and that thing seemed to be movement. He began
to trot through the bush. As he got more and more agitated he went more and more swiftly. He accepted Dingo
as the leader, and as the heat and smoke grew worse, he
struggled on after the wild dog. Then he heard the terrifying crackle of flames in the trees as the fire caught up
with them; the flashes of heat seared his hide as burning
sparks and windblown twigs touched his body. The fear
felt by both the horse and the dog emphasized their dependence upon each other, their essential loneliness.

They came to a little rise and plunged down it. At the
bottom of the slope a small creek had been dammed
naturally to form a pool beneath a jagged, overhanging
rock. Dingo plunged into the pool and looked back over
his swimming shoulder for Brumby to follow him.

Brumby, eyes wide and white-rimmed with fear,
stepped into the water and waded in until he stood
beneath the great overhanging rock. There Dingo
crouched on an underwater rocky ledge so that only his
head and the wet hair along his back, floated upright by
the water, showed above it.

There they stayed while the flames swept down to the
creek bank and were driven back by the water. They
filled the air with their fiery breath and Brumby snorted
and gasped his fear as he breathed the burning heat into
his lungs. Flames ran along the edge of the creek devour-

ing every leaf and blade, every dry stick and old fallen log as it went.

Brumby plunged about in the pool as the flames menaced them, crackling and roaring, but did not try to leave the water. Sparks leapt the water at its narrowest part and flames roared along the other side and over the top of the rock that protected the two below it. By now they were not alone; every small and frightened living thing crowded into the pool. Some swam wildly about, but more drowned and floated in a pitiful tangle on the surface.

Except for the discomfort of the brown fiery particles, the smoke and the heat, the two big animals were unharmed. A kangaroo which had leapt into the water at the last minute before the flames could catch it pushed its tall tail against the rock on which Dingo lay, but he took no notice of it. Brumby learned a valuable lesson in seeking sanctuary, a lesson that was on another day to spell the difference between life and death for him.

When the flames died down and the roaring and crackling of the fire ceased, Brumby came out from the chest-deep water, Dingo slid from the ledge and swam after him, and the tall, water-soaked body of the kangaroo followed Dingo to the bank. There it sat, squeezing pieces of water-soaked fur in its small hands, while Dingo shook the loose water from his coat.

The air was acrid with smoke and all the visible world was charred and blackened, unpleasant in the animals' nostrils. Brumby stepped carefully for a few yards, lifting his hooves high above the hot blackness, sniffing at it and jerking his head back. There was nothing to eat on this ground, so he and Dingo set off to cross the area of the fire, which was a wide one. The ground was still hot and Dingo's unprotected pads suffered, while Brumby's hooves protected him.

The Brumby

When the rains came the horse and the dog returned to the fire-swept country again, drawn by some instinct, perhaps some hint of sweet greenness brought to them on the wind. The grass was sweeter and richer for the burning. The heat of the fire passing over the ground burst seeds that had lain dormant for many years; germination had been waiting to begin from just such a fiery accident.

Dingo's instincts were alive to the danger of man's dwellings, and he influenced Brumby, who had no such instinct to guide him. In the freedom of their wide range Brumby had come no nearer to man's houses than during the unfortunate time when he learned that it was unwise to be in the vicinity of fighting bulls. But while that experience taught him to treat bulls with respect, it also taught him that mere post-and-rail fences were no barrier to his wanderings.

It was the need for grass that eventually drove him nearer to man in spite of Dingo's uneasiness. Brumby was a two-year-old, a stallion of immense power, swift and strong and implacably wild. All his freedom from instinctive fear of man could not make him forget his terror as a yearling, the shouting and whip-cracking of men, the wild race that had separated him and his mother from the herd. Even the tragic death of his mother was somehow associated in his mind with man. Perhaps he dimly remembered his coltish games with Myall and Moonlight, until their loss had the same association.

So while necessity sent him to graze nearer and nearer to man's homes – for the reason that man always chooses the most fertile land, land that yields the only available food in times of drought – the sound of a shout, the crack of whip or rifle, even the distant barking of dogs always sent Brumby plunging back into the scrub again.

Sometimes on moonlight nights Dingo would go off about his own affairs, especially if he heard the strange double-calling of one of his kind. Yet he always came back again to roam with his friend, to sleep near to him through the hot noontimes, to play with him at night.

Brumby had never known the delight of cultivated food, and it was the sweet, cool scent of a hayfield that came near to being his undoing. One night he came on a small patch of ground that had been fenced in rather badly by posts and five strands of wire. Brumby came out of the scrub and stood sniffing at the strange smell of wire, while Dingo wove through the grass near him in an agitated manner which Brumby ignored.

Brumby touched the wires impatiently with his nose and pulled his head away quickly, then thrust it back again under the top wire and gave it an impatient bump. The thin, taut wire hurt his nose and he pulled back snorting angrily. Then he tried pawing at the wire with his near-side hoof. The lower wire creaked and sagged to the ground, but the other wires remained taut. He seemed no nearer entering the beautiful green enclosure then before, and he might have given up in disgust.

At that moment a soft, excited whinny came from the far side of the little paddock, where a rough building loomed dark in the moonlight. Whether Brumby knew that it was a mare in that old wooden shack, or whether he only knew that after so long one of his own kind was near to him, it is impossible to know. He backed from the wire fence, lifted his head and gave a whistling call in response. He began to move about in an agitated way, approaching the wire fence and backing away again as though he recognized it for the highly dangerous thing that it actually was.

Again the mare gave her call. Brumby, his eyes shining and his nostrils flaring, stamped at the hateful wires. The second wire from the bottom snapped, the back-lash of it caught him on the fetlock before dropping to the ground. He stamped impatiently at the next wire and his hoof went over it, leaving him with his shoulder against the two top wires and the third one pressing against the inner side of his leg. He leaned and strained and the wires became dangerously loose. When he tried to pull out from the loose wire it caught and sent him plunging back, cutting his leg to the bone. Some inner intelligence prevented him from struggling wildly and crippling himself fatally on the slack wires. He stood sweating with fear and impatience, puzzled, trying to work out what he could do to free himself.

A horse without Brumby's intelligence would have been finished, possibly crippled for life, but Brumby, instead of pulling away, leaned forward. The top wires held. His leg hurt him badly, but he was too excited to notice it very much. He lifted the cut leg and stepped back from the imprisoning wire.

The wild horse moved a few restless steps up and down the fence and came back to the mutilated span that had so nearly trapped him, and he considered it. He lowered his head and thrust it under the lower of the top two wires; it gave a few inches but it was not high enough for him to walk under it.

Slowly and deliberately he lay down and rolled his body over the two wires that lay on the ground and under the two taut top wires. When he was clear he rose to his feet and shook himself and sniffed at the wealth of succulent green feed around him, but did not stop to eat. He moved towards the old shack where the mare was stabled.

A sloping rise lay between the shack and the farmer's small house that was almost a mile away. The sound of barking dogs was so distant that it scarcely amounted to a sound at all. Brumby ignored it as he ignored Dingo, who had watched his conquest of the fence shivering with nervousness all the while, though for no more specific reason than that man and all his works are suspect to all wild dogs.

Dingo followed Brumby through the wire fence, crouching low and creeping through the green wilderness belly to the ground, out of sight, except that his path was marked by the agitated waving of the green tips as he passed through the stems.

Brumby reached the shack and whickered eagerly, and the mare answered him. It was an old shed, and he moved round to the front of it which gave on to a wide paddock fenced by the post-and-rails kind of enclosure that Brumby had met before.

Whickering and stamping, Brumby pawed at the wooden slabs. He could hear the mare stamping on the hard earth inside her stable. Presently he lost patience and reared up and pounded his hooves on the ancient slabs. They trembled and shook, but held. This was too much altogether for Brumby. He backed near to the shed and kicked with his hind hooves, landing them with shattering impact against the old wood. Like some double battering-ram he pounded the wall, and the shattered planks fell away. A sleek brown mare, made nervous by all the noise, stepped outside.

All would have been well except that in his excitement Brumby failed to notice that the far-away continuous barking of a number of dogs was getting louder. Tom Lugg, the cocky farmer who owned the cultivated patch and the mare, also owned a pack of nineteen or twenty dogs which he used for hunting. At night he tied or shut his dogs up so that they would not use up their energies hunting for themselves, and he was used to their hungry barking. The dogs, never fully fed, un-

used to human kindness, severely punished for any disobedience and used to long, gruelling hunts, were fast,
savage, and tireless, a formidable lot, dangerous in the
way that a wolf-pack is dangerous.

It was more than an hour before Lugg decided that
something must be disturbing the dogs and that he had
better investigate it with them. Savage as his own dogs
at being dragged out in the middle of the night, he loosed
them with curses and indiscriminate kicks which broke
the swelling chorus into sudden yelps and howls as his
vicious foot found its mark. He called them to heel and
they knew better than to disobey. He stood for a minute,
a slouching, dirty-looking man with a stupidly brutal
face, and he counted over his dogs to be sure that none
of them had slipped away.

They were a raw-boned, mongrel lot. Half a dozen of
them were various crosses of Kelpie, a breed that had
been recognized about 1870 for use with sheep. The pure
Kelpie bred back to where a crossbred bitch with half-
dingo blood had mated with a smooth-haired Scotch
collie. Her pups had first been called Kelpies, and they
became of value because their mother won the first sheep-
dog trials held at Forbes, N.S.W. Lugg's Kelpies were
hunters, not sheep-dogs, but they had the stamina and
intelligence of their breed. Then there were several great
kangaroo dogs, powerful and fast, looking like giant
greyhounds. A Bluey, a type of cattle-dog, ran with this
motley lot and the rest were made up of mongrels whose
blood was too mixed for them to favour any special
breed; they were simply big, wolfish dogs, bred to kill.
The dingo cross had not been confined to the Kelpies.
Often one of the dogs escaped from the pack to mate
with a dingo bitch, and the wild dogs' blood added to the
stamina and savagery of the pack.

Lugg had no affection for his dogs. He valued them

only as butts for his bad temper and bullying, his love of domination, and he used them only for his own advantage and gave scant attention to their needs. It was to his advantage to encourage tough killers to lead his pack. He could watch a stronger dog set on a weaker or injured dog and kill it, without interfering or showing the slightest pity for the under-dog.

That night the dogs were all eager to go, their bellies too empty for sleep. They looked towards the slope so that it was not difficult to see that whatever agitated them lay in that direction. Lugg, who had heard faint sounds like the cracking and falling of big branches, thought that might be what had disturbed the dogs. If his sleep had been disturbed for nothing, then he would see that the whole pack paid for it. But perhaps it was something more; after all, they were used to hearing boughs break and trees fall, without going on in this way.

Lugg sent the dogs to heel while he walked up the long rise in the moonlight towards his patch of feed and the shack in which he had put the bay mare. Even his brutality could not stop the yaps of excitement coming from the massed dogs.

Brumby, the shattered shed behind him, stood before the bay mare, whickering and sliding his head along her sleek neck, giving her small nips that made her whicker and squeal back at him. Suddenly she drew back and lifted her head. Through the clear night air came the sound of the approaching dogs.

Dingo ran to and fro at his friend's heels, urging Brumby to move, but Brumby arched his neck and pranced back to the mare, shaking his intelligent head, displaying his powerful body and springy natural paces for the benefit of the mare.

Then there was a sound that he could not ignore; it was a shout, the sound of man. Forgotten memories flooded back; he was a colt again, galloping in a frenzy of fear while voices like this shouted at him and whips cracked and snaked across his back. He drew away and turned to face in the direction from which the shouts were coming.

A dog came running over the crest of the rise, baying loudly. Still Brumby hesitated. Dingo slipped through the fence and watched from the thick edge of the scrub as the whole pack of dogs came pouring over the hilltop, racing ahead of their master who was still out of sight and some distance down the hillside, so that only his repeated shouts reached Brumby's startled ears.

The mare trotted away, only slightly alarmed, for she knew that the familiar pack was not after her. But by now Brumby's alarm was catching; he pawed the ground and snorted, and the leading dog streaked towards him. Just as it was about to leap for the stallion's throat, the horse rose and struck downwards with his flint-edged hooves. The dog screamed its agony and without another look Brumby broke into his powerful, rocking gallop and went straight for the post-and-rails fence. The fact that he had moved out of the wire enclosure gave him a chance. He cleared the rails, and seeing the golden-red hindquarters of Dingo ahead, he instinctively galloped after him.

Lugg came over the hilltop in time to see a magnificent white stallion leave the ground and sail over the fence with his dogs in pursuit. He let the dogs go and stopped before his shed, cursing. The door and the heavy planks at one side of it were completely shattered. He looked around; the reason was plain, and at least he still had his brown mare. If he had not come along it was probable that she would have been taken off by the stallion.

'Some great brumby comin' after the mare,' he grumbled.

When he looked further, he found the broken and twisted wires in the fence and marvelled that the stallion had not crippled himself. He stood for a moment listening. Already the dogs were too far away to be heard. He gave an ugly smile. 'The pack'll pull 'im down – ef they don't, then I'll git 'im meself one way or t'other,' he muttered, and trudged back to his home.

At first Brumby galloped swiftly through the scrub, then his wire-cut leg began to trouble him. On clear ground the kangaroo dogs might have caught him, but the big, swift dogs could not get a clear run to use their speed. The scrub was a tangle of dry, sloping and lethal sticks to pierce a fast-running dog's chest, so that the speed of the pack was lessened by the obstacles even more than was the speed of the stallion, who crashed through the tangle, doubling and twisting and now and again catching a glimpse of his golden friend running ahead of him.

Brumby, thinking he had out-run the pack, dropped to a trot, and Dingo slowed up too, his tongue lolling and dripping from the side of his jaw as he turned his head over his shoulder and looked back at Brumby.

The yapping of the leading dogs came clearly on the wind. They drew nearer and Brumby began running again. He was tired now and his leg bled badly. He crashed on, again and again slowing down to listen. The dogs were always following.

Full-fed, and given the right country, Brumby could have out-distanced the pack except, possibly, the giant kangaroo dogs. But he had not fed well for some time, and while the scrub was even more of a handicap for the dogs than for the horse, it also prevented Brumby getting one fast, sustained run that would draw him ahead of his pursuers. He had lost a lot of blood from the deep cut in his leg, and was limping badly.

The stallion and the pack went many miles into the wild no-man's-land that edged Lugg's property. Dingo too was running heavily. He could have slipped off into the bush and so evaded the dogs, but he would not leave his friend and continued to lead the horse towards the country they both knew, although if they had been overtaken his destruction was certain.

They passed over the ground where the bush-fire had so nearly caught them. Ahead of them lay the creek with its deep pool beneath the overhanging rock, and once again Dingo made straight for that.

The yelping of the dogs was very near when Brumby, weary but still full of fight, recognized his whereabouts. Straight as an arrow he followed Dingo, and as they had done on the day of the bush-fire, he plunged into the pool and waded beneath the rock, turning his hindquarters to the wall so that he faced the bank upon which the dogs would appear.

Dingo swam the creek, reached the other side and shook himself before he disappeared into the scrub again. By whatever means of communication there was between wild horse and wild dog, Brumby knew that he was not to follow Dingo then. Perhaps his instinct told him that Dingo would be as much at a disadvantage in deep water as would be the pursuing pack; whatever it was Brumby stayed in the pool, the coolness lessening the bleeding of his leg. He sipped an occasional surface mouthful of water, and waited, his ears flickering nervously, his thudding heart quietening, a fighter ready to face his enemies.

They came almost at once, a score of fierce, hungry killers. Two of the giant kangaroo dogs reached the creek-bank first, their jaws slavering, their great barrel chests heaving in and out after their long run. Behind them came the yelping chorus of the mixed pack, running, pushing, eyes glaring, teeth bared in their realization of the nearness of blood, their one thought the tearing of living flesh, the chance of perhaps, feeding full before their master beat them away from their prey with whip, kicks and curses. In all their hunts Lugg was always close on their heels riding one of his horses; they did not understand that now they were on their own. They were imbued with the feverish urge to kill and to eat, eat good red flesh, Brumby's flesh, before it could be taken from them.

Brumby waited for them, moving his hooves a little, standing firmly on the hard bottom of the pool. The water was a little lower than it had been at the time of the bush-fire, but still deep enough for the largest of the dogs to have to swim to reach him. It would have no grip for its paws and therefore no ability to use the strong muscles of its haunches to launch itself for the kill. Now they would have to conquer by weight of numbers alone.

Undaunted by the water, the pack launched itself into the pool until the surface was crowded with silent, swimming heads. Brumby whistled his wrath, reared upwards until his crest touched the projecting roof of rock that jutted out above him, and he brought his flailing hooves down again, cutting and battering the leading dogs, sending a fountain of water everywhere.

When his front hooves touched the bottom again to get his balance for another assault, two badly shattered dogs swam feebly for the bank and dragged their broken bodies out on to it, while three corpses floated on the water.

The water was still patterned by heads, hiding the swimming bodies that regrouped themselves for attack. With the corner of his eye the stallion saw several dogs leave the pool at one side, then screaming his rage he struck again with his off-hoof. One dog went under, its skull crushed. Two others reached his shoulder and their fangs gripped his flesh. With a squeal of rage Brumby turned his head so that his solid teeth met in the skin of one of the dogs and he pulled it from his shoulder and flung its limp body upwards. It fell into the water and floated away.

The dogs were all around him and he leaped and stamped to throw them off. Somehow he twisted his neck and gripped the back of a dog that was hanging to his throat, and the dog's spine crunched, it went limp and its jaws ceased to grip. Then, fighting like a fury with hooves and teeth, Brumby charged out into the water, flailing his hooves, biting and squealing, sending up fountains of water to fall back drenching his hide and slapping on to the surface of the pool.

On the lip of the rock above his head, the three dogs that had left the pool crouched, but they never leaped on his water-darkened back because a red-gold bullet hit them. Two tumbled into the pool and Brumby struck them down to stand with his hoof on the body of one so that it was both crushed and drowned. Dingo fought the third for agonized minutes until the body of the dog lay there. The wild dog unlocked his terrible jaws and looked down at the corpse of his first kill in the lust of battle.

The pool was a shambles. All that was left of the pack were five injured dogs swimming desperately for the bank. Brumby charged at one of these, and seizing it in his teeth he lifted his powerful neck up and down until the dog flopped as if it had been made of rag, and Brumby flung it from him. It fell between bank and water and lay motionless.

The last four dogs went staggering off into the scrub and Brumby walked out of the water with arched neck and high-stepping hooves and shook himself. He was bleeding from a dozen savage bites, his silver hide was marked and torn; he had had his first battle against living and unequal odds, and he had won it, though not without paying the price in many painful wounds.

When, three days after their defeat by the silver stallion, the four remaining dogs of Lugg's pack crawled home, they got no sympathy from their master. He showed his displeasure by brutal shouting and kicked the beaten creatures. He was furious at losing the rest of his pack and vowed vengeance on Brumby.

Lugg knew that in time the wild stallion would return and look for the mare again. He brooded for a long time on the reception he would give him. He had just decided to sleep in the stable and to shoot the wild horse out of hand, when Dugan came riding up on one of his lean, harried horses. The two men had something in common if it was only their stupid brutality.

Inside the dirty kitchen-living-room of his ugly little wooden house, Lugg put the tin kettle on the greasy blackness of the wood stove. He and Dugan sat down on one of the rough wooden benches that took the place of chairs, and they drank tea from their chipped enamel mugs as they talked. Dugan sucked his tea down in loud gulps before he lifted his unshaven face to ask,

'Wot about that mare of yours? Wanter sell 'er?'

'No fear. Not fer a bit any'ow –' and Lugg launched forth on the tale of the white stallion. Dugan was interested.

'A white brumby, didjer say?'

Lugg nodded, and Dugan thought quickly. This might be his chance to get himself a real horse. What if it was wild? He'd soon belt the stuffing out of it. 'Never seen a 'orse yet yer couldn't tame with a fourteen-foot lash, properly used, an' used fer long enough.' He went on talking round the subject; he was not going to let Lugg see he wanted the stallion in case he got the same idea himself.

'Wondered wot 'appened ter yer pack o' dawgs.'

Lugg cursed and spat on the already filthy floor.

'Just fer that I'll fill that brumby full o' lead. I'll 'ave ter shoot th' kangaroos this year, there's only four dawgs left – an' two of 'em's 'alf crippled – think I'll knock 'em on the 'ead, not worth usin' good bullets on 'em,' he added callously, and Dugan nodded agreement.

'Yer say th' stallion was white?'

'Yairs. I only saw 'im jumpin' th' fence, fine-lookin' 'orse.'

'Might be one o' th' brumbies we ran orf the Meehan place about a year ago, some of 'em was white an' I remember a couple of good-lookin' colts was in th' 'erd.' His face took on an even more unpleasant look and his thickened shoulder twitched. 'Got th' run goin' meself an' didn't git nothin' outer it. Bob Johns got 'is two mares back, but I didn't git a look-in.' He thought for a minute and added cautiously, 'This ole nag I'm ridin's just about fit fer the bone-yard. Seems a pity ter shoot a 'andy 'orse like the wild stallion, better ter catch an' geld 'im if 'e's any good. Ef I give you a 'and, we could dope out some wayer catchin' 'im, an' I might throw in a few bob as well.'

His hard, cunning little eyes peered at Lugg over the dirty tin mug. The idea appealed to Lugg. He thought to himself, 'One quick shot and it'd be all over,' and that wasn't revenge enough for the loss of his pack and the breaking of his wire fence. No, Dugan had the right idea, if he played it carefully he might get himself some dough into the bargain. So he agreed that Dugan could have the stallion in return for his help in trapping it and for 'a coupla quid'.

The two men walked towards the shed in which Lugg

kept the mare, the four miserable-looking dogs following. The ones that had been hurt worst were in bad shape, for they had been unable to hunt their food and their master did nothing to help them.

Near the stable lay a pile of rough-cut railings. The trunks of trees felled in the bush had been split roughly in four, to be cut later on into five-foot lengths, when Lugg extended his fencing. Dugan looked at these with thoughtful eyes. It would be a lot of hard work, but – well, if the wild horse was as good as Lugg said he was then he could be sold for a lot more than two quid plus the work of helping Lugg. He said nothing to Lugg about the possibility of reselling the horse, in case he went back on his bargain and either demanded more money or wanted the stallion for himself.

Finally they agreed that the best thing to do would be to take ten-foot lengths of the split logs, bury them upright firmly in the earth and put in the same thickness of cross-rails, making a small, high yard beside the shed. Then, with the back of the shed reinforced by some of the logs and a heavy gate at one side, they would have a trap from which even the wildest brumby stallion could not escape. It would be too small for him to be able to take a run and jump it – and too high as well – and it would be stout enough to resist an elephant.

Both men sweated through the hot days, digging post holes and carrying the heavy timber, and at last the yard was finished. From inside the shed a rope controlled the heavy gate, letting it drop to imprison the stallion. Then they went to where Brumby had already torn and loosened one span of the wiring. They pulled the wires back, leaving an opening, experimented with the heavy fall of the gate for a few times, and were highly pleased with themselves.

While all this was going on the mare had been tied

to the side of the house at night. She would probably be in season in three weeks or so, and they argued that they could expect Brumby to come back then. They would take her back to her old quarters in the shed, but until there was evidence of Brumby being around, the heavy drop-gate would be kept lowered. When he was really eager, coming every night, trying to find a way in, the gate would be raised and when he entered his prison would close about him.

Everything went according to plan. Two nights after the mare had been put in the shed, heavy hooves had trampled the earth outside the fence. Two nights after that again the men walked up to the stable before moon-rise. They put a halter on the mare and raised the heavy fall-gate. Then they settled themselves to wait. The dogs were shut away, nothing disturbed the quiet of the night about them except the far-off cry of a mopoke and the rustling noise of small animals moving through the grass.

An hour, two hours went by. Then the movements of the mare, her restless hooves, the way she raised her head and gave soft, excited whinnies, told them that the white stallion was drawing near. Presently they heard an answering whinny coming from the scrub. Lugg chuckled, both men peered through cracks in the slabs.

They saw a splendid silver creature step from the darkness of the scrub like some prince of light, scarcely pause at the break in the wire fence and come walking across the patch of green feed with beautiful, free movements, his intelligent head held high, a Samson coming to his Delilah.

The men kept perfectly still and the solid white side passing across the cracks in the planks blotted out the moonlight. Brumby came round the end of the stable – now! Lugg's hand tugged at the rope and the heavy gate crashed down almost touching the big hindquarters. The silver horse jumped and backed against the high, strong fence, then he raised his head and screamed his wild challenge.

Dugan chuckled, 'Got the so-and-so – let's git back an' git some shut-eye. 'E's safe till mornin'.'

Lugg looked sullen. ' 'E's a real beaut,' he said grudgingly, thinking he had been tricked into trading this splendid animal for a couple of pounds.

As the two men emerged from the door of the stable, the white stallion reared, pressed against the railings. These things were men; he hated men. He reared again, pawing the air, and squealed with rage. Then his hooves came down on the ground, he shook his head angrily, snaked his neck and charged. The two men scattered and probably saved their lives – and Brumby's and the mare's too, for had the horse cut them both down, he and the mare would have died of slow thirst and starvation, for there was no one to free them from the strong trap in which they found themselves.

Brumby hesitated. The two men walking together had seemed like one entity to him; now they were split into two he was undecided which to charge first. That instant's hesitation sent the flying forms of the men scrambling over the high fence.

When Brumby chose his victim it was Dugan, and the man was on top of the fence and about to drop down the other side. Brumby reached up and clamped his solid teeth on a fold of his trouser leg. The material was old and filthy and the piece tore away, otherwise the horse would have pulled him back into the yard and savaged him. The energetic tug with those strong teeth nearly dragged Dugan off the fence, but he hung on, and as the piece of cloth tore out he fell sprawling down the outer side of the fence.

Lugg, who was already on the ground outside, made

matters worse by laughing. Dugan rose, looked at his tattered trouser leg and muttered what he would do to the horse in the morning, then limped angrily after Lugg.

Left alone, Brumby trotted a few steps about the enclosure. Out of the scrub Dingo crept and sat on his haunches a few feet away, tongue lolling, worried and uncertain about what had happened to his friend.

In the morning Dugan came over the top of the hill, carrying rope and stockwhip. Lugg was with him. Brumby's movements became more restive. The horse craved water, but his hatred of man made him forget his thirst for a time.

After that the man and the horse battled for three days. At the end of that time, crazy with thirst and hunger, the splendid stallion was gaunt with suffering, but he remained unbroken. Lugg drawled that they might as well shoot him, he would be no good even if he was broken if this went on much longer. So Dugan, not out of compassion, but simply from the desire to get some return for his two pounds in one way or another, gave the horse a drink and a feed. Brumby drank the water avidly after a few preliminary backings-away from the bucket. He dipped his nostril deep in the water, then blowing and choking he ended by knocking the bucket over and pawing at it with his forehooves. He was more wary of the food, and only ate it when it was left with him all night.

Next day his splendid wild strength had come back. At night Dingo came and sat near to him, watchful and worried, fading into the scrub with the dawn. That day Dugan and Lugg improvised a sort of crush. Working from outside the yard, they pushed heavy logs across a corner of the yard near to the drop-gate. When that was done they lured Brumby into it with a bucket of water. The tissues of his huge body still sadly lacked moisture.

Once he was in the crush, they fastened Brumby's wild head with ropes to get the bridle on him, and after that the saddle. Because Dugan was afraid of this great pale beast, he felt nothing but brutality towards him, but he did not want to go far enough to spoil the price he meant to get for such a splendid horse.

He decided to try Brumby once himself, now they had the saddle on him. Dugan did not like the idea of the ride at all; but Lugg's sneers drove him to mount the horse. When he was in the saddle with the huge captive body hunching and quivering beneath him, Lugg raised the gate and pulled out the logs that formed the barrier of the crush.

Brumby, his soft mouth cruelly hurt by the bit, outraged by this thing that had been tied to his back and by the final insult of the man who mounted him when he could not move head nor hooves, stood quite still for an instant, not realizing he was free. When he did realize it he rocked back on his great haunches, plunged from the crush and began to buck.

Dugan tried to wrench Brumby's head around and to force him into the open paddock. The bit tore the soft corners of his mouth and blood and saliva dripped from it, but he refused to answer the iron pull on the reins and he bucked the buck of a real champion, plunging all over Lugg's cultivation. Brumby did not waste time pig-rooting as a lesser horse might have done. He lowered his head, humped his body and leapt into the air, bunching his hooves beneath him above ground, and giving that sideways twist in mid-air that few men can sit.

Dugan could not sit it. At the second buck he rose high in the air against the clear blue of the sky, the reins were torn from his hands and he fell heavily on to the waving fronds of green that padded the earth.

Lugg ran into the patch of cultivation and shouted

and cracked his stockwhip as Brumby propped and wheeled, utterly dazed, utterly outraged. Instinct prevented his charging at the wire fence; he turned, and back in his mind he remembered the post and rails he had cleared so easily before. He wheeled, Lugg's whip snaked out, and frenzied with rage and the desire to be free, the horse saw an opening and rushed through it – he was back in the enclosure and the heavy gate fell behind him. Dugan picked himself up and swore, Lugg smiled maliciously.

'My word, that's a real buckjumper you've got there!'

Dugan looked at him with surly eyes. He was bruised and shaken, but the ground was soft and padded by the high green growth. For the first time Lugg remembered that his cultivated paddock had been crushed and torn up by the bucking horse and he started to grumble about it. Dugan looked at him furiously. 'Aw, shut up!' he grunted, humped his heavy shoulders and started back to the house, walking with a more pronounced limp than usual.

'Hi! Ain't you goin' ter take the saddle and bridle orf the –'

'When I'm ready, an' that ain't yet,' Dugan snapped back at him and Lugg shrugged his shoulders and followed him.

Back and forward Brumby moved. The hateful things on his head and back distressed him. He bent his head and pawed at the bridle. It held fast. Then he twisted his body sideways and tried to scrape the saddle off against the rough railings. Hour after hour he scraped and rubbed. First the saddle swung round under his chest, and that frightened him as though some evil animal clung to him. His continual moving and scraping eventually broke the girth, the saddle fell to the ground and he trampled it. Then he went back to the bridle. His mouth hurt and made him more savage than ever. Again and again he bent his head and pawed at the bridle. Finally the forehead strap slipped over one ear and from then on it was easy to pull it off. Finally the bridle, too, lay dusty and trampled beside the saddle. Dugan never went back to the yard that night; he never gave a thought to the thirst and suffering of the horse he had trapped.

A strange horse was tied to a tree when the two men came in sight of the house. It belonged to a drover on his way to pick up work round the Macintyre River. He camped at the house, and during the evening he mentioned that he had passed George Rutland's Buckjumping Show which was making its way to Conway's Flat.

'Usen't to be a bad show,' Lugg said. The newcomer nodded his head.

'Not upter much now. Can't git th' 'jumpers, George told me. A few lousy-lookin' mokes was all I saw. Still, George's made plentya dough in 'is day, an' when 'e strikes it lucky with a good'un 'e'll be all right again.'

This piece of news gave Dugan an idea. He questioned the drover as to exactly where Rutland might be found, and he calculated that the Show ought to be passing along the main road about five miles away sometime during the next morning.

Soon after dawn Dugan, stiff and sore from the fall Brumby had given him, rolled out of his bunk, and got himself a plate of corned beef and a billy of tea. Then he walked up the rise towards the old stable.

Brumby saw him coming and his eyes flashed fury as he snaked his neck and screamed his challenge at the hated man. Dugan, safe outside the heavy railings, wasted no time. He looked at Brumby with a critical eye and felt a mean satisfaction when he saw that the gloss had gone from the horse's silver hide, that the wild eyes were bloodshot, the mouth torn and bleeding, so that the long streels of bloody saliva had caked on his chest. His rubs stuck out of his gaunt side and the big muscles, usually bunched so smoothly under his satiny hide, were knotted now just beneath the skin. Dugan thought that though the horse had fallen away so much since his capture any real bushman would be able to see what a fine savage brute he would be in condition. All the same, the better he looked the more money he would fetch.

Dugan dragged the trampled saddle and bridle through the fence, then fed and watered the horse lavishly. The gentle brown mare cropped the grass of the paddock outside the enclosure, and when Dugan left she came to the heavy railings and whickered and pushed her soft nose through them to touch Brumby's torn and bloody one. Dingo, too, watched Dugan leave. Then the wild dog came silently out of the scrub and lay for a little time near to his friend.

Lugg and the drover were moving about when Dugan returned. He caught his horse, which was in better condition now that it had had a few weeks' rest, and saddled it, calling over his shoulder to Lugg,

'The brumby's mauled my saddle an' bridle about, so I've took your spare. I'll be back later.' Without further explanation he jumped on his horse and rode off. The drover looked after him.

'Wonder where 'e's orf to? Grumpy sorta cove, ain't 'e?'

Dugan chose a flat stretch of road on which to wait, a stretch that had plenty of room on either side of it, and where water was about a hundred yards away in a billabong that sparkled in the sunlight. Here there was plenty of room for the Show to stop, and they would be ready to pull up for tucker any time after noon.

He settled himself under a coolibah beside the road,

feeling pretty sure that the Show had not passed already; in that case there would have been fresh wheelmarks and hoofmarks, and there were none.

After an hour or so he heard the sound of rolling wheels, of hooves and the jingle of harness, and men's voices shouting to each other. The first wagon carrying gear and drawn by four strong, nondescript horses came in sight. Rutland was driving and at the curve of the road Dugan saw a light cart following, driven by one of the hands. Then four horsemen came in sight. Among them he recognized Rutland's two half-caste riders who were known all over the state, and who led a team of five buckjumpers. Dugan noticed with satisfaction that the drover had been right, they looked a pretty poor lot. He stood up and hailed Rutland.

'Hi, George!'

Rutland's answering 'Hi!' was not very cordial, but he pulled up his horses and said,

'What're you doin' about here, Dugan?'

'I've gotter proposition fer you — a real buckjumper. You'll be tuckerin' about now, won't yer? Well, pull up 'ere, there's plentya room, an' we'll talk it over.'

Rutland looked undecided. 'It'll want to be a pretty good proposition.'

'This un's the real McCoy,' Dugan answered confidently. Rutland shrugged his shoulders and turned his team on to the side of the road, shouting to his men that it was tucker-time.

The two half-castes took the horses to the little billabong that showed through the trees and watered them. They tethered and hobbled them well away from the rest of the show, and came back carrying the billies they had taken with them. These dripped with slimy greenish water, and the men proceeded to make a fire on which to boil them.

Rutland asked Dugan no questions until they had eaten their slabs of cold meat and hunks of damper from the hastily mixed loaf that had been cooked in the ashes of the fire. Then he lay back on his elbow and took out his pipe, while his men cleared things up.

'Now, what's this about a buckjumper?'

'Well, I trapped a brumby –'

Rutland looked disgusted. 'Oh, a brumby,' he said in a disparaging voice. 'They're never any good, can't buck, tame too easy an' don't have the stamina.'

'Not this one. It's one o' those that useter be on the Meehan place.'

'I heard about them,' Rutland nodded, his interest revived. Dugan launched into a description of Brumby. When he had finished, Rutland, his face not giving away the extent of his interest, asked coldly,

'What d'you want for the stallion?'

He laughed when Dugan mentioned a figure, and then the two men really sat down to bargain. Rutland said he was not prepared to waste his time looking at the horse if the price was not right. Finally he nodded.

'All right – but mind you, only if the horse is what you crack him up to be. Anyway, I'll take a look.'

He called to his men to set up camp, and then walked over and had a few words with his foreman and with the two rough-riders. Then he had one of the spare horses saddled for him. The rough-riders carried ropes, stockwhips, a spare bridle and a halter, and hobbles, and they led a couple of sturdy old-stagers, heavy animals with draught blood in them, horses that knew everything that was wanted of them. All these preparations showed Dugan that Rutland was at least prepared to buy the buckjumper, and Dugan felt confident he could sell him.

They reached Lugg's place about four in the afternoon. The drover had gone and Lugg was away, so they rode straight on up to the old stable. Dugan watched Rutland's face when he saw Brumby, but Rutland was too old a hand to change expression. Nevertheless when he saw the magnificent development of the silver horse, the bared teeth and the rim of white around the wild eyes, he was impressed.

The half-castes knew their business. They were small, thin men dressed in dusty trousers and shirts. One wore elastic-sided boots but the other was barefooted. Under the brims of their old felt hats their dark eyes were as wild as Brumby's own. They had small, narrow hands, narrow hips, and they walked like fighting men, balanced on the outer edges of their feet. They were called the two best rough-riders in the state, these two brothers, who, on the ground, looked about the size to ride a lively pony. On horseback they had all the magic of their people, and for sheer ability to ride an outlaw there is no race in the world to touch the Aboriginal.

Without wasting time in talking, the two dusky men got ready for one of them to ride the untamed creature that screamed and reared, rushing to attack with bared teeth and flailing hooves. Using the improvised crush in the corner, they drove Brumby into it. Then the bridle went on and the bit pressed against the torn mouth. Over the bridle Jimmy put a strong halter and he held on to the long end, mounting one of the old-stager horses that were used for the work.

Rutland raised the gate as Charlie dropped from the railings on to the bare, outraged back of the silver horse. Brumby charged out of the gate, and in spite of the man on his back and the hampering bridle and halter he leapt wildly into the air, his four hooves dangling, his great back arched. The whole animal was completely relaxed in the air, which gave his rider no inkling of which way the twisting movement at the peak of the buck would need the countering movement of his own body, if he was to ride it. The twist came and the wild horse threw his rider into the air to land sprawling on the ground a few yards away.

Immediately Jimmy Ellis and the stolid work-horse braced themselves while the fallen rider picked himself up, his work done; the Boss had seen what he wanted to. He and the two riders knew that here was a great champion, a horse that was a true buckjumper in the lithe, athletic way that is given to few horses. Those few possess a gift that cannot be taught; they are equine athletes and are rare and valuable to man.

Freed of his rider, Brumby still bucked and fought the bridle and the long halter rein. Jimmy held on to him, while the old horse he rode knew exactly how to keep the right tension on the rope.

Charlie Ellis, his light body scarcely shaken by his fall, moved quickly to the rails and took down the rope he had left there. He jumped on to the other horse and cantered to the far side of the leaping, fighting white stallion. In five minutes the two Aboriginals had the stallion trussed up between the wise old work-horses. The bit was out of Brumby's mouth and a muzzle put in its place, so that his terrible teeth could not menace the two horses flanking him closely. Even his great strength would not let him overthrow two horses almost as strong as, and infinitely more experienced than, himself.

All the noise and confusion frightened Dingo. He crept silently to the edge of the scrub and crouched behind a log as he watched his white friend being led away between two other horses. He turned his intelligent head to one side as he saw the two men on the ground, and his sensitive ears flicked at the chink and rustle of money passing between them.

Then Rutland mounted his horse and rode off after his men. Dingo saw the hated Dugan limp downhill out of sight. He whimpered a little deep in his chest, and for a while he ran parallel with the riders, watching his friend's ceaseless and unavailing struggle against his bonds, saw him always overpowered and forced to walk to another's will. After a few miles, Dingo gave up and disappeared into the scrub.

That night, where Brumby was hobbled and tied, sweat-covered from his exertions and with every fibre of body and mind filled with furious frustration, the far-off, intensely sorrowful sound of Dingo's cry came to his ears. Whether or not he knew that it was the voice of his friend no one can say, but for a second the horse ceased to struggle, and his intelligent ears went forward; again the cry came out of the night. Then it was answered from some distance away and the double chorus went on, easing a little the loneliness of Dingo's heart. If he had lost the object of his strange friendship, at least there was comfort to be found for him in his own kind. But it was not this way for Brumby. He could not even have the consolation of knowing that he was at least lucky to be away from the brutal Dugan, for Rutland, although a harsh man, was not a brute. No man, however, would be allowed to try to become the friend of the wild horse, for in his loneliness lay the factor that kept his implacable savagery alive.

The comfort Brumby might have felt that first night, from being herded with his own kind at last, was taken from him by the manner of his herding and from all that had gone before it. With every muscle of his strong body, every instinct of his wild mind, he resented the horses about him; slaves of man, these creatures smelt of man, got their being from man, were subdued and driven by him.

His gaolers, the two strong half-draughts with years of dominating wild horses behind them, knew how to deal with him. Just as a young wild elephant is roped between two old tuskers, so Brumby was roped between the work-horses, and he gave them no easy time of it. He was muzzled and could not bite them; he was tied and could not move far enough away to kick or to rear up and strike them, but he could and did give them heavy blows with his head and his muzzled mouth, even though these hurt him too. They were forced to drag his great weight every step of the way. He could make the going very tough for everyone around him, and he did.

George Rutland and his two rough-riders were heartily sick of coping with Brumby by the time they reached camp, and the Boss was already regretting his bargain. Then, when he looked at the splendid silver horse and saw the temper and spirit in those brilliant eyes, he could not altogether regret his purchase.

One look at Brumby's gaoler-horses told the Boss what they thought about things. They were dripping with sweat, bruised about the shoulders and heads, tired and sulky. No one knew what the Ellis's thought. It would be their job to ride this flashing-eyed demon, and moreover they must ride him without making any attempt at friendliness.

Special reinforced halters were fastened to each side of Brumby's head and then stretched to the trunks of two trees with about eight or ten feet between them. Into the centre of the space between the trees the two old-stagers dragged him. Hobbles were fastened to those two lethal front fetlocks and the muzzle loosened so that the horse could shake it off himself.

Then the tired work-horses were unfastened and led away. In an instant Brumby tried to make a dash for it. Hobbles were something he knew nothing about. He plunged forward, and fell. Struggling wildly he tried to rise, beating the air with his chained-together front hooves. Every time he tried to stand up he overbalanced, and his struggles sent the muzzle flying through the air. Brumby stopped his furious movement and the Ellis's looked at each other and grinned.

'Plenty brains, eh?'

Brumby thought for a minute, rolled on to his stomach, and putting his front hooves carefully on the earth he managed to get on to his feet. He tried a step forward and nearly fell again. The ropes allowed him little latitude. Strong as they were, and made of rawhide, that has plenty of stretch in it, too much slack would have meant he could break them with a sudden jerk. As it was, his struggles strained the ropes, and the leaves on the stout trees to which they were tied shook wildly with his first titanic outburst, sending a flock of screaming cockatoos out into the sunlight from their midday siesta.

Brumby was dark with sweat and trembling from the intensity of his exertions. He took the couple of small steps his hobbled hooves allowed him, keeping them together and moving with little bucking movements that made the chains clink. Jimmy Ellis nodded his head.

' 'E's got th' idea now,' he said.

Brumby stood, his sides heaving, his nostrils opening and closing like the petals of two crimson flowers. Wariness had replaced the fury in his eyes. This was a new situation, new insults were being heaped upon him. Very well, he would learn how to cope with them. His wild heart thudded steadily and a small wandering breeze began to dry the caked sweat on his side.

When Charlie Ellis brought him a bucket of water, and a second bucket half-filled with dry feed, Brumby went wild again. With a squeal of rage, a surging of his muscles, he reared up against the halters, and one snapped. Feeling himself free on one side, he plunged about on his hobbled hooves, rearing upwards like a great tower, his manacled hooves beating the air as he fought to get at the two men who were trying to feed and water him.

Twenty yards away the Boss and the men of the Show stood in a line, watching their new property. One of the men ran forward with his rope, and the noose settled around Brumby's neck. The man took a hitch round the tree, but not before Brumby, with a scream of rage, reared above Charlie Ellis, who had slipped forward to make a grab for the overturned buckets. Quick and lithe as a snake, Charlie twisted his body from under those menacing hooves, but as Brumby brought them down in a striking movement, the off-hoof caught in Charlie's dilapidated old shirt and ripped it from his back. The half-caste moved out of range and shrugged his shoulders; the hoof had barely touched his skin, but had left a raised red weal down his back. He watched Brumby stamping on the shirt, plucking at it with his teeth until it was pounded to shreds. The Boss spoke.

'You boys watch out for that stallion, he's a killer. Look what you're doing and hand him the buckets on a pole.'

Brumby found that the rope around his neck allowed him a certain amount of play, and he pulled against it. The noose tightened and he shook his head furiously and pulled again. It tightened still more. The horse coughed and threw his head up and down. When he relaxed he found the noose loosened. It was plain to the watching men that he was considering this new problem and was reaching his own conclusions.

'Yer can almost see that 'orse think!' one of the watching men said admiringly. The Boss looked grim.

'He's brainy an' he's savage – and I wish I'd never touched him. You boys remember what I said. I don't want any accidents.'

As long as the men stayed away from him, Brumby rested quietly, only his incessantly moving ears showing that he was always on the alert. The moment anyone came near him the plunging and whistling began again. At last there was something he could fight against beside the great adzed posts that had made up the yard in which he had first been trapped.

It was late in the night when Brumby heard another horse's hobbled jingling and the thud of its hooves nearing him. Even tied and hobbled as he was, Brumby was not an enemy to be despised. Standing quietly, muscles taut, he waited until the big black came almost up to him, its ears flattened back, its neck snaking, moving in little jumps on its hobbled fore-hooves.

The black horse came closer, and Brumby's head shot out; his teeth fastened in the black's crest in a crushing bite while he reared up a foot or so and brought his hobbled hooves down on the black's fetlock. The black screamed with pain and rage. Then the black and silver necks were snaking out in quick, feinting movements that sometimes passed each other as swordblades might have done, but sometimes ended in cruel, tearing bites.

The Ellis's, sleeping rolled in their blankets a little away from the campfire, sprang up at the first real squeal, the sound of thudding hooves, the rattling of hobbles, and they drove the two horses apart, tethering the black well away from the stallion. The Boss loomed up out of the shadows and swore when he saw his leading buckjumper lamed and torn and unfit for work for a week or more.

'That silver brute'll bring us nothing but trouble,' he muttered, and stamped off back to his tent.

The Brumby

In the three days that followed Brumby fought his captors every inch of the way. He slowed up the progress of the Show considerably, so that they arrived at Conway's Flat a day later than was advertised. Sometimes the stallion walked quietly along for a few miles and everyone's spirits rose. Then, for no apparent reason, he would go fighting mad and make the work-horses drag him along. He never accepted the fact that the ropes that bound him, and the hobbles that hampered him, were stronger than he was himself.

Part Three: The Leader

Although Joey loved Moonlight with all his heart, she was just a little disappointing to him. She did not love Joey nor anyone else, at least she never seemed to, though in a way she trusted the boy. He was able to handle her, to feed and groom her; he never attempted to ride her, but he did teach her to lead. She took almost a full year to recover as much as she ever would from Dugan's treatment of her. When she was rising three she still had a pronounced limp, especially when she walked, but at a gallop it was little noticeable. Her injured eye had healed but was not a pretty sight. The white eyeball was set among bad scarring that gave her delicate skull a grotesque look on one side. Joey's heart mourned over the thought of what she might have been, an exquisiteily lovely little mare but for her limp and her mangled head. The aloof spirit of her wildness never left her. Dugan's brutality had formed a barrier between the animal and man through which no one could break entirely.

Jim said they would not attempt to breed from Moonlight until she neared her third year. Joey used to dream gloatingly about the foals she would have one day, small animals as beautiful as she would have been, foals to be the progenitors of horses with bloodlines of his and his father's own choosing.

Joey himself had not changed much in a year except that he had grown taller, which made him appear even thinner. Flash, who had settled down to the unvarying kindness he found at Joey's hands, sometimes became almost playful. Life had been hard from his earliest remembrances, the playfulness that is the heritage of most foals had been denied him; so now, in a mild way, he entered into his belated childhood. He carried Joey backwards and forwards to the Bretts' for his lessons from Rowena, and sometimes he gave a mild shy or a shadowy curvet which delighted Joey. The old horse had very little asked of him, and in return he got full measure of the love he had been denied all his life; he was well content.

Often Joey, as he sat around listening to his father yarning with other men, wished passionately that he could see one of the buckjumping shows they described. When his father came home one evening and told him that there was to be just such a show at Conway's Flat, and that he was taking him to it, the boy was wild with excitement. Joey had never been to a picture show, nor to a theatre, and he could not imagine anything in the world as exciting as watching a buckjumping show. When he rode to his lessons the next day, Geoff was sitting in the kitchen talking to Rowena. Joey burst in, his face crimson with excitement.

'I'm goin' to the buckjumping show!'

'Well, fancy that!' Geoff and Rowena looked down at his excited little face, asking, 'Is it George Rutland's Show?'

Joey nodded, and a lock of tow-coloured hair flopped up and down. 'Yes, I think that's what Dad said.'

'I heard he had trouble gettin' 'jumpers, but anyway you'll like it!'

'You bet I will!' shouted Joey.

The buckjumping tent, enclosing the stout circle of fencing that had originally been built as a ring for just such shows, was set on a flat piece of ground by the river. Rutland was a showman who tried to turn everything to his own advantage, so he sent on an advance party with orders to build a second small, but very strong ring. Over this the spare tent was erected.

This enclosure was destined for Brumby only. From it to the big tent was a kind of strong alley-way leading to the crush at the entrance of the big ring. Rutland was not at all sure how Brumby would behave in the ring, and he was determined to take every precaution. As Brumby could make him, so he could break him if there was any carelessness. The silver horse was dragged into the round yard beneath the tent, fighting like a fury against being put beneath this strange and terrifying cover.

Once he was there, the people from the little township and those that came in from round about paid sixpence to see 'The Savagest Buckjumper on the Face of the Earth'. This not only brought in a little money, but it advertised Brumby, and most of all it advertised the Show as having new blood.

Even in the small yard Brumby's splendid proportions prevented his looking his great size or showing the weight of his big body. He seemed very tall, a wild, silver killer. His tremendous muscles were packed under his tightly stretched, shining hide in perfect symmetry; he was in splendid form, not only because he received the best care, but also because his continual fighting and struggling against authority gave him the exercise his great frame needed. No show-owner wants to see his horses 'broken' in the usual sense of the word; the art of the business lies in keeping the horse at the peak of his aggressiveness.

Rutland walked around his Show to see that everything was shipshape. He stopped to speak to the two

Ellis's as they walked out of Brumby's tent, carrying the empty feed buckets. Charlie Ellis pushed his old felt hat back on his head and took the cigarette the Boss offered him. He was the one who usually spoke for both of them.

'How d'you boys feel about the ride you're goin' to have?' Rutland inclined his head towards the tent. Charlie Ellis grinned.

'It won't be the first time we got chucked off, Boss,' he said cheerfully.

'Well, watch yourselves, step lively when he chucks you. I'll have Ted and a couple of the boys ready with ropes to keep him off. I don't have to tell you if you stay on the ground you'll get savaged.'

Charlie nodded. 'We'll be O.K., Boss, don't you worry none,' he said calmly.

Conway's Flat and the surrounding country could only produce a handful of spectators, far too few to make the show pay, but as they had to go through it on their way to more heavily settled districts, Rutland wanted to give his Show as it would be later on, for now it had become a try-out for Brumby. That night would prove the buckjumper's worth, and give them an idea of what they could expect from him.

All Rutland's men were keyed up before that first performance. A thin trickle of people came from the little township, walking, riding, driving in buggies and sulkies and occasionally wheezing along in their old cars. Some of the audience had made a journey of thirty to forty miles. Everyone knew Rutland and most of them liked him and were glad to hear that he had at last struck it lucky and found a really good buckjumper.

Outside the big round tent, horses, buggies and cars were dotted about the river bank. Inside the tent there was no real seating. At the back were a few roughly erected posts with rails let into them, so that people could perch on these and see over the heads of those who crowded about the ring. The dull, smoky light came mostly from blazing flares and acetylene lamps. The flares flickered and smoked whenever a gust of wind touched them.

Joey and Jim came into the tent and mingled with the crowd. Jim had been late home from work so that they only arrived a few minutes before the Show was due to start. Some of the men already there greeted Jim and motioned him to take his boy to the front so that Joey would be able to see. Joey clung to his father's hand. He was not used to being among a crowd and he was frightfully excited. Across the ring he saw Geoff Brett's red face and shouted and waved at him. Brett waved back, calling,

'Yer'll wanta give Flash back to me when you see those horses!'

'No, I won't!' Joey yelled. 'I wouldn't change Flash!'

Geoff elbowed his way round the ring and stood beside Jim.

'They tell me Rutland's got a real beauty of a 'jumper.' 'Who's ridin' it?'

'Oh, I s'pose one of the Ellis boys, they're real hard doers, no one to touch 'em about 'ere.'

Jim nodded and looked down at Joey.

'Watch the gate of the crush, son, that's the way they'll come in – oh, here's the first horse now.'

It was the number two buckjumper of Rutland's string of five that came into the crush, the number one being still out of condition after his bout with Brumby. The number two was a half-hearted performer and it looked as if they might have to put a flank-rope on him to make him buck. Eventually Charlie Ellis succeeded in making him perform by dint of much shouting, digging his bare heels into the horse's ribs and slapping its flanks with his old felt hat. The men around him began muttering scornfully, and although Joey watched, his blue eyes wide with excitement, thrilled by the whole scene, he was inwardly a little disappointed himself.

The next horse was even duller. Then a murmur went through the crowd. Many of them had paid their sixpences to see the big silver horse and they made knowing remarks to their neighbours who had not. The second buckjumper left the ring and the babel of voices grew louder. Joey saw Jimmy Ellis climb to the railing on top of the crush and he knew that the half-caste rider was waiting for the horse that people were talking about.

Rutland leaned against the stout railings across the ring from Jim and Joey. The air was smoky from the flares that blazed and flickered alternately, filling the tent with moving shadows that swept across the brown, intent faces of the little crowd as they swayed closer to the ring, their rough voices making a monotonous pattern of sound.

The Boss of the Show looked around. The future of his Buckjumping Show rested on the way that Brumby performed that evening. Rutland allowed his dreams to expand; the high post-and-rails that formed the ring became, in his imagination, surrounded by a sea of faces, not just the handful he was looking at now. The night air seemed to fill his ears with the hoarse shouting and yelling, the tremendous enthusiasm of a big bush crowd that had never before seen anything to equal his wonder horse.

Movement in the narrow lane that led to the ring brought him back to the present. He heard the heavy thudding of hooves, the stallion's wild, piercing whistle. A rush of wind seemed driven before the great silver body as the horse charged into the ring, eyes flickering red within their sinister white circles, mane tossing, neck arched. The furious, driving energy in the huge frame seemed to swell the barrel of a chest as the horse entered with ears flattened and teeth bared, and the people of Conway's Flat got their first glimpse of Brumby. Above their cries of admiration and the clapping of hard palms that sounded like rain on a tin roof, came a piercing, childish voice.

'It's Brumby! Oh, it's my Brumby!'

Jim Meehan looked down at his son. He had drawn him a little away from the rails, as all the crowd stood back when Brumby made his spectacular entrance; it was safer that way. Joey's small face glistened with sweat and excitement and there was joy as well as tragedy in his eyes. Brumby was a captive, but at least he was alive, vitally alive, charged with life as a bolt of lightning is charged with electricity; just to know that meant a great deal to Joey.

Somebody shouted, 'Look out!' Jim grabbed his boy, and he and those around them moved hastily back as Brumby paused in his mad dash round the ring, looking for escape, for a weakness in the railings. Then he stopped and wheeled, rearing so high that his mighty chest seemed as tall as a snowy cloud in the sky, and he gave his furious, screaming cry while his long legs lashed the air. The moment those lethal hooves touched ground, hooves trimmed by rocks and hard earth, by the stony bottoms of creeks, made strong as flint by continuous contact with fallen ironbark and coolibah boughs hardened by sun and air, a slim, ragged figure in shirt and trousers and wearing dirty old sneakers slipped with the furtive speed of a wild thing from between the railings behind the horse. Looking more like a shadowy blur than a man, Jimmy Ellis gave his quick, cat-like run and sprang on to the back of the great horse.

The insult of this small, light figure on his back sent Brumby back on to his haunches, to rise again, pawing the air and shaking his head. Jimmy was still there when the stallion came within an ace of rearing over backwards. He dropped his forehooves to the ground and began to buck. He charged forward, rose in the air with his four legs limp beneath him, and seemed to fling his body sideways like some giant snake; it was a twisting, unrideable movement.

The half-caste rider rose in the air and crashed to the ground near where Rutland stood. A rope shot out and almost before the mighty hooves hit the ground the injured rider had been dragged through the fence, and Rutland bent over him.

In that second Charlie Ellis made the same rapid forward movement and sprang on to the horse. Rutland, torn between anxiety for his rider and the desire to watch his horse, glanced at the ring. Something shot from the top of what appeared to be a seething white cloud. Rutland stood up and swore. He saw, too, Jim Meehan push his son into the hands of the man next to him and in a blur of speed dive under the lower rail, grab the fallen man and spring back with him while the scream of the stallion and the sound of his forward plunge, the rush of that enormous, sweat-streaked body, sent a shiver of terror across even his hardened nerves.

Joey had no time to realize his father's awful danger before Jim was back with him again, gently lowering the unconscious Ellis. Then he heard Rutland's voice shouting,

'Look out! Get back everyone!'

'Back, Joey!' Jim still held the unconscious man as he pushed Joey back to where the crowd was scrambling to get out of the way. In that moment it seemed as if

Brumby had gone mad, that not only madness but the strength of some evil spirit was contained in his colossal body. The horse flung himself from side to side, reared and brought his hooves crashing down on the railings again and again, piercing the air with his whistling screams. Even the stout wood could not stand the hail of battering blows and with a splitting crack the top rail sagged. The silver body rose, thrust the top rail into two pieces with his chest, charged over the lower rail, and plunged through the scattered crowd. Any who were not out of the way quickly enough were knocked right and left, and those by the open flap saw the great ghostly hind-quarters of the stallion disappearing into the night. Geoff Brett broke the silence.

'That wasn't a horse you had, Rutland, that was a devil!'

A murmur of assent came from the men around him. Joey knew he should have been frightened, but he hadn't been; he knew that he should be sorry for the damage Brumby had caused, and he was, but over and above this was an inner joy that Brumby, *his* Brumby, was free again.

There was no doctor and it might be some hours before one could be found, so several of the bushmen did what they could to help. Most of them were rough but efficient bush doctors, and while they could not be certain what other injuries the two riders suffered, it was plain that Jimmy Ellis had a head injury, possible rib-fractures, and was badly bruised, and Charlie had a broken leg. Both men were unconscious. Fortunately none of the crowd through which Brumby had galloped were more than bruised and frightened.

When everything that could be had been done for the two men, Rutland turned wearily towards his own tent and said to Jim and Geoff,

'Come an' have some tea, you must need it, I know I do. Both my riders are badly injured, but if it hadn't been for you, Jim, one of them would be dead – pounded by that devil's hooves and shredded by his teeth.'

Joey walked beside his father. After all the excitement he felt very sleepy but he tried to keep awake. He stood leaning against his father's knee while the three men talked, and he munched drowsily on the raisin-filled lump of cake that Rutland handed him. Jim glanced down and saw his half-closed eyes, and he smiled a little. Joey was like all bush animals, used to going to sleep almost at sundown. He lifted the little boy on to his knees and Joey leaned against his shoulder and fell asleep. Geoff looked at the child and said,

'You'd better let me take him home in the sulky, Jim, he can sleep on the floor. I drove in because Rowena wanted a few things brought home. Joey can use them for a pillow.'

Jim nodded. 'Thanks, Geoff, I'll lead Flash.'

Rutland sat down wearily, on a seat made from a piece of carpet nailed between the folding legs of a stool, and lifted his mug of hot tea.

'Well, that's settled it,' he said gloomily. 'I thought I had the buckjumping sensation of Australia.'

'You had that all right,' Jim drawled.

'I know, and I wish I hadn't.' He shook his head and then went on, 'There's something devilish about that horse. I've had 'im less than a week; he's worn out my two best work-horses, he injured my number one buck-jumper so's he won't be any good for weeks. Now he may have killed both my riders, anyway neither of them'll be fit to work for months, and it's only luck he didn't kill some of the crowd – an' I thought I'd got him cheap!'

'What did you pay for him?' Jim asked.

'Twenty quid – from that bloke Dugan, never did like 'im, I oughter've left him with the horse.'

'Dugan, eh?' Jim looked thoughtful, then asked, 'Well, what're you goin' to do now, go after 'im in the mornin'?'

'No fear. I know when to cut my losses. I wouldn't have that silver devil back, not if someone brought 'im to me in chains. I've had enough.'

'I dunno whether my kid's right or not. He thinks the horse is the yearling from a herd of brumbies that useter live on those mountains on my place. Joey calls them "his" 'erd an' it nearly broke his heart when Dugan got up a brumby run and drove them away. That silver devil, 'e might be anything from a three- to a six-year-old, I'd say, wouldn't you?'

'About three or four I'd think, it's 'is size makes him seem older – and I don't ever want to look in 'is mouth to prove it!'

'Well, if 'e's a three-year-old he just might be the same one. Joey calls him "Brumby", like it was a word for "King" or somethin'. Anyway, I don't suppose we'll ever know now.'

'No, I don't suppose so. The stallion's gone bush, an' as far as I'm concerned he can stay there until the brumby shooters get 'im, if they ever do.'

'Rutland, it's my kid's birthday the day after to-morrow. You know how kids are. You say you don't want any more of that stallion – let's call him Brumby – well, how about sellin' 'im to Joey for a coupla quid? At least that'll be somethin' back on your twenty?'

'Sell 'im to the kid? I'll *give* 'im to the kid and welcome, for all the good it'll do 'im!'

'No, wait a minute. Joey believes, and I think he's right, that some day that herd'll come back to the mountains. When they do I'll 'ave no more brumby runnin'.

You see, neither Bill nor Geoff nor I 'ave the money for
fencin' so our places are wide open of any stock that's
movin' about. If that herd comes back I think I'll 'ave
trouble with Dugan wantin' to run them again. He come
off worst last time, an' a bill of sale from you just might
help, because I think he'll try to shoot Brumby like 'e
shot the old leader, for no reason at all except that 'e's a
bad tempered so-and-so.'

'If you want to get even with him you'd better let
him have the horse,' Rutland said drily, and Jim
smiled.

'Joey wouldn't feel that way.'

When father and son left Rutland's tent, Joey slept on
peacefully, and as well as carrying him, Jim carried in
his pocket a bill of sale which identified Brumby as the
horse Rutland had bought from Dugan, and certified to
the sale of that same horse to Joey Meehan for two
pounds.

The cool night wind dried the dark sweat out of
Brumby's hide as his frenzied galloping settled down to a
steady pace. His hooves, crossing the brown-skinned
beauty of the plains, beat a steady bayonne that sang of
freedom to his sensitive silver ears. He galloped on effort-
lessly, going instinctively to the north, his wild, easy
movements making no barrier of the furry, formless
darkness about him. Over his proud head the Milky Way
flowed through the sky, and freedom sang in his veins
and charged the air that filled his powerful lungs.

Brumby slowed to a trot, then to a walk, then he
seemed to stroll along, bending his head to sniff at the
grass and to tear up a mouthful at his own lordly pleasure. The taste of the growing grass, in place of the richer
mixture in his feed-bucket, tainted by human hands, was
to him as the quick, living kill would be to Dingo after

the cold, tasteless meat of captivity, lacking the quiver of life, the exciting smell of flowing blood.

When dawn came Brumby was nearly thirty miles from Conway's Flat. When the early light shivered about him he trod on sandy soil near water and he stopped and rolled, wriggling his broad back against the sand, kicking his legs and snorting with pleasure. Then he rose, shook the loose sand from himself and went down to the creek to drink, sucking the water through his teeth. When he was no longer thirsty he pounded the surface of the water with his hooves in a kind of monstrous playfulness that sent fountains of water over his chest and shoulders.

When the sun, hot from its birth, poured down, Brumby stood by some supplejack trees and switched his tail, wrinkled his hide and dozed peacefully as any domesticated horse might have done, except for the incessant movement of his ears. He was oblivious of the damage his brief brush with civilization had brought on all who were around him.

The mere fact of his freedom, at first so tremendously exciting, soon assumed its accustomed place and was taken for granted. But now Brumby knew something of man's way, he knew what loss of freedom could mean and he was a warier and a wiser horse in consequence.

In a few days the driving urge of all wild stallions animated him, the urge to form his own herd. He began to acquire his wives with comparative modesty, by coming like a great white ghost out of the night to where pack-horses grazed a little way from a smouldering fire and the sleeping forms of their owners. The two mares were hobbled, but Brumby's brisk nips on the rump of one mare, his quick, bustling pushes, shoulder-to-rump, as he drove the mare before him into the thick scrub, made her snap her hobbles and in a few seconds both horses disappeared into the night.

Brumby acquired two more mares in this buccaneering fashion before he came across a small herd of brumby mares and foals, and challenged the stallion. This herd had begun when the death of Yarraman had broken up the herd with which Brumby had run as a yearling, but of course he did not know this, nor would it have mattered had he known.

The other stallion was a dark chestnut lacking Brumby's look of high breeding, but he was a big, strong horse, twice the other's age and with that many years more experience of fighting. He was a horse that bore the fighting blood and plebeian qualities that spoke of the prepotency of the blood of his sire, Yarraman.

The shrill, high-pitched whistling of a stallion calling to his mares came to Brumby where he moved through the scrub at the rear of his own newly acquired mares. He turned towards the direction of the sound and saw the strange herd as the mares came up from watering, followed by the stallion which had led them to drink and which, now that their thirst was appeased, moved into a strategic position behind them where he could watch his harem returning to grass.

From the straggly tree edging the creek-banks, dry ground stretched away to the darkness of a scrub several hundred yards away. There, a hundred yards from the bank, in the centre of the bare ground, the leading mares saw the motionless figure of a great white stallion. Brumby stood with his head raised, and the swelling arch of his crest outlined against the sky. His own mares moved at the edge of the scrub and the mares belonging to the other stallion turned their heads and whickered. The big chestnut heard them and pounded up the bank, forcing his herd to the left, seeing Brumby waiting, motionless as a statue.

The chestnut turned, as the etiquette of such things

demanded, sending his mares along the bank for fifty yards or so, keeping himself between them and his challenger. He trotted briskly along the line of mares until he considered them safe, then he turned and went towards where Brumby stood until perhaps twenty yards was between himself and the silver horse.

Then each fighter worked himself up into the required pitch of fury. Dust billowed upwards from their pawing hooves, making gauzy, golden globes about them in the sunlight, blurring the outlines of their two bodies.

Like a white flame blown by a gust of wind, the silver horse sprang from his misty covering towards the other, and the chestnut met him with snapping teeth, flint-edged hooves and eyes red with hate.

The tangled manes tossed and teeth clashed as the horses reared chest to chest, heads darting, front hooves striking, their movements a gigantic and deadly dance. In the dusty nimbus they spun around, wrestling and weaving, hooves smashed against muscled bodies, hides were torn and blood spurted.

The fighting of bulls is a thing of weight and brute courage, it is charged with primeval brutality and noise. The fighting of stallions is a far more terrible thing, for it brings pride to the kill, intelligence and will and a refusal to accept defeat even in the ultimate agony of being beaten down, driven off, or killed.

Blood poured down Brumby's sides and from his neck the flesh hung down in shredded red ribbons. Things might have gone badly for him but for an accidental blow that happened in the wheeling and twisting of the other's body. The sharp edge of his hoof struck against the stifle of the older horse, pulping the bone and causing him to arch his loins in agony above his useless leg.

This was Brumby's chance and he took it, charging in with his great weight, screaming, biting, kicking. The

other stallion staggered on three legs then overbalanced and fell. In an instant Brumby was on him, hooves pounding the life from his body, while his great teeth instinctively tore at his throat and his life ebbed away.

Rage died down in the victorious stallion. He stood above his fallen enemy, head high, neck arched, his own blood dripping downwards and mingling with his foe's. The wildness died from his eyes and his laboured breathing became calmer. Throwing his head high he whinnied his victory, giving out a sound as different as is the snarl of a fighting dog from the purr of a contented cat. He wheeled and trotted, stepping high, and going towards the stranger's mares he drove them into line and sent them towards his own waiting mares.

They, in a world where might is right, probably gave no thought to their fallen leader, but transferred their allegiance to his skill, his courage which had kept them free, his cunning which kept them fed and watered, to his successor. Some day, in his turn, he might yet lose them to another stallion, perhaps a grandson of his own in all the power and beauty of youth.

That summer was hot and dry and the herd needed all Brumby's bush-bred cunning to keep them alive. The heat was intense, even the whirlwinds, the willy-willies of the Australian plains, seemed touched by it. Little circles of lazily moving dust, dry twigs and leaves began to gather on the open ground here and there, only to settle inertly on the earth as the exhausted puffs of wind faded and died. The creeks seemed tired. The mud and stones between the shrunken pools were barely wet, and the sluggish current had ceased.

Brumby captured his herd at a time when it took all his native cunning, all his inherited pride to enable him to keep it together now that it was of a size that was entirely outside his experience. He ruled them on the edge of fear and led them to food and water in a land that was sucked dry by the burning sunlight, a land where water is seldom plentiful at the best of times, and where the blades of grass are withered and dry in those sparse areas where they can be found at all. Everywhere the once succulent roots had lost their moisture and become no more appetising than so many lengths of knotted string. It was as though the world had died and its flesh shrivelled beneath its dry brown skin so that soon the bones of the land must burst through the drum-tight covering.

The herd grew thin and restless, and Brumby moved about it, a gaunt shadow of his once splendid self. But he never relaxed, never lost his wariness against man, other stallions or his own mares, never forgot the thousand dangers of his wild homeland. He led his herd or trotted warily behind them as the occasion demanded, driving them before him to where his instinct suggested there might be feed. Attempts at straggling were literally nipped in the bud; mares and foals were required to keep in a formation which Brumby could manoeuvre at will. Disobedience brought the laying-back of the stallion's ears, the angry light to his eyes, the dangerous snaking neck movements and the sudden prop, swing around, and thud of hard hooves on the culprit's ribs.

Where there was dry feed, feed that is more sustaining for a horse on a hard journey than any he can get from green and juicy grass, Brumby found it; he seemed to possess another sense which told him where to find water, perhaps in the dried-up bed of a creek or trickling among the rocks, or in an old water-hole where the mud had hardened to become white, cracked and seamed by sunlight, mud that spread out of the damp darkness of the central patch like a saucer of rough-dried cement.

A billabong, once a hundred yards long and half as wide, an oblong bowl that in rainy times held six or seven feet of water kept fairly fresh by rain, became in droughty times a mere tub of water perhaps two feet deep, from which every living creature in the area must drink. This bowl lived up to its Aboriginal name of 'dead water'; it was dead itself in its static shrinkage, and filled with the dead bodies of bush creatures.

The herd went towards the billabong, led by Brumby. Beneath their hooves and stretching around them the small brown-furred bodies of rabbits pressed on at sunset to find the water they too must have.

Before the herd topped the little rise that led up to the banks of the billabong, their eyes, filled with no more realization than that possible water lay before them, took no interest in the sky that was dotted with eagles, great wedgetails spanning seven or eight feet of the sky through which they soared and circled on motionless wings, making invisible algebraical patterns through the air. Every few seconds an eagle stooped downwards and at the end of the stoop a squeal of pain cut the air. Most of the rabbits were too crazed by their need for water to become conscious of the shrilling of the wind through the pinions of the feathered missiles that stooped and struck. At least death had come in a swifter way than by the myxamatosis that was soon to destroy their hordes.

Sometimes a thirsty rabbit became conscious that death was diving upon him and he leaped away, jumping sideways, crouching, running, but it was never any use. The angle of the final rush altered, and the rabbit was swept upwards after the additional horror of a few more instants of suspense. It was seldom an eagle landed; if it did it lurched along on its white feet for a yard or two and then took to the air again.

The hooves of Brumby's herd were as lethal to the

rabbits and other small game pressing towards the water as were the eagles. They left a broad swath of crushed and mangled rabbits, but thousands more hopped or ran over their dying brothers, surging forward implacably to where the heavy air held the scent of water.

It was strange that the water itself should be the predominant scent in a world where the stench of carrion-torn flesh, of stinking mud filled with rotting fur and flesh, seemed reekingly stronger. The number of soft-furred bodies beneath the horses' hooves was doubled and trebled at the edge of where the water had once been. Now it was liquid mud except at the very centre, and all around was piled body on struggling body. The stronger rabbits, the late-comers among them and the foxes, emus and dingoes ran across a heavy carpet of dead rabbits with only a living top layer. Trodden into the ground, the first-comers who might have drunk the water and lived were smothered and crushed by the mass of their fellows.

The centre of the billabong was filled with water-logged bodies and the bigger animals scratched and clawed in an attempt to get through the bodies to what water might remain beneath the sodden mass of fur. Big animals like the horses simply trampled on this carpet of death, and they nosed and pawed and perhaps got a mouthful or two of the thin, stinking mud. Nevertheless, all the mares crowded after Brumby. They reached the very eye of the pool and stamped and pawed, nudged and snorted, finally turning away in disgust to fight their way back to the bank.

Somewhere on the stinking wind came the sound of low thunder and the dejected mares raised their heads; faint whinnies sounded in answer. The thunder drew nearer. Brumby led his mares to the parched ground, edging a scrub where the leaves on the trees hung dark and sapless; he stood for an instant, wild head high, flaring nostrils drinking the storm-scent that came to him on the wind. He whinnied and began a brisk trot round his herd, marshalling them, encouraging and exciting them, in his own way telling them to be of good heart for rain was coming.

It came, a quick, violent shower that drenched their bony bodies. As the puddles formed on the ground the heads went down to the water and sucked it up. Like gleaming steel rods the rain fell. As Brumby circled his herd his white body shone through the rain. He paused to stamp and whinny; his mares became playful and nipped each other, squealing with joy, and the foals, who had no memory of the feel of rain on their rough little bodies, felt the urge to gallop and whistle, to indulge in mock battle and to imitate the pawing and squealing of their elders.

The sharpness of the storm abated, but a steady rain took its place and the herd quietened down, turning their rumps in their immemorial way towards the beating of the rain.

Almost overnight it seemed that the grass sprang up, tree-barks sweetened, the stale billabong filled and over-flowed, small creeks tumbled down and swelled the rivers, and the animals' ordeal by drought was over – for a time.

It was a happier, more serene little boy who went back to his lessons, his daily routine, after Brumby escaped from the Buckjumping Show. The bill of sale which made Brumby his own was duly presented to Joey for his tenth birthday and was received as ecstatically as his father had anticipated.

More than ever Joey talked about Brumby with a proprietary air. Of course most of his talking was done to Flash and Moonlight, but Joey didn't mind that. He talked to Rowena, too, as she moved about the small wooden house, her long, old-fashioned skirts flapping against her bony ankles.

Joey never wavered in his belief that some day the brumby herd would come back to the mountain, and he was quite certain in his own mind that it would be Brumby himself who would lead them back. His dreaming eyes saw himself taking the halter off Moonlight. She would run to Brumby – and she would return to himself of course. In due time she would have a foal, the first of his and his father's great herd to be, a foal that would carry the matchless blood of his sire, Brumby, and would be called 'Florian'.

Almost every day Joey rode up the mountain. He left Flash to feed and climbed to his vantage point to see if the herd had returned yet. Every day he dragged the wooden stool in the hut over to the wall, climbed up, and lifted down the painted tin box Rowena had given him, a box that had once held fancy biscuits. He opened the lid and took out the bill of sale that made Brumby his very own horse. He read it carefully, folded it and put the whole thing back again. He always gave a lingering look at the painted lid which showed an apple-cheeked little girl leaning over a gate. She had a bunch of grass in her hand which she offered to a rather shapeless cream pony. Joey didn't think much of the pot-bellied pony, deciding that it must have been a poddy, but he liked the little girl and the rose-covered doorway of the cottage behind her. It fascinated him; it was not much like the world in which he lived, and he liked to speculate on what such a home must be like inside.

He worried during the drought, wondering if his brumby herd was getting feed and water. He hoped that if the drought continued they would find their way back to the mountain corral, for there were patches of nourishing grass still there, shadowed by the rocks. Every day when he crossed the gully and looked up the slope ahead of him the yellow grass rippled like a sea of pale gold, and the hard, silken shininess made a faint melody when the breezes blew among the dry stalks and sent them murmuring together. His hard bare feet brushed through the grass-stems as he went upwards, hoping that particular day would show him his herd. The herd was never there and he gazed with longing eyes across the thirsty cracks below that sliced the dry plain.

Then the rain came. Joey's heart was a patient one and the little flame of hope in it burned steadily as he stood watching the changing surface of the plain, watching the water trickling through the great cracks that would dry out quickly as the heat of the following sun turned them again into the colour of brick-dust.

The storm beat around his bare head and his feet squelched into the ground. He rode slowly home, enjoying the soaking of his body. When he reached the hut the rain had already swollen the wood round the window and door, and the corrugated iron roof that had cracked and creaked in the heat now thundered beneath the falling rain.

Jim was not quite as patient as Joey in his belief that the wild herd would return, or perhaps he was just more practical. He came back early from work one evening as coolness descended, and found Joey in the stable brushing down Moonlight's pale and shining coat. Joey greeted his father joyfully. He pointed at Moonlight, saying proudly,

'Isn't she beautiful? Like a silver gum in the moonlight, smooth and shining.'

Jim nodded. 'Yes, she's a good-lookin' mare an' it's time she had a foal.'

Joey looked shocked.

'Oh, but how can she? Brumby isn't back yet,' he said earnestly.

'Then we can't wait for him.' Jim spoke firmly. 'Anyway, if you let her join the herd you might never get her back again. Now listen, Joey, I've made up my mind. I rode back past Bill's place an' he says I can take her over there while he's got that big chestnut stallion from Larrakia – Geoff's takin' his three mares over an' it's a good chance.'

Joey put the currycomb back on the wall and turned away. Jim looked at the droop of his thin little shoulders and felt a sudden irritation. Jim was tired; it had been a long day. Joey ought to have been pleased at his news. It was time he got over being sentimental about Moonlight. Normally it would cost twenty-five guineas to take Moonlight to the chestnut stallion and that was out of the question. Now, because he was to collect the stallion on Bill's behalf, Moonlight would be served free. In his exasperation he did not go into the details with Joey. This time Joey must do as he was told; he would be pleased enough when he saw the foal. Jim gave his shoulders an irritated hunch, turned round and walked towards the hut without saying anything more.

Joey looked after his father, then turned and gazed at Moonlight with miserable eyes. Flash was outside, and Joey jumped on his back and rode towards the mountain. The little boy prayed fiercely. Rowena told him that real prayers were always answered. Well, now was God's chance. If prayers were answered then he would see the brumbies back in their mountain retreat – now. He hurried Flash, still keeping up his praying, his blue eyes determined. He rode down the gully and part-way up the hill. Then he jumped off and ran on upwards, scrambling and slipping as the hill became steeper, until he reached his vantage point. Still he refused to look across the mountain because he was determined to make one last, one frightfully strong prayer, determined that God should have one last chance to answer before he tested his prayers, and looked.

He opened his eyes. In the evening light, a blend of gold and grey, the mountain was completely deserted. Joey's faith in prayer was jolted but he clung to it stubbornly. He peered across the plain, peered at the dark line of trees on the far side, and suddenly his eyes filled with hope. He was certain, certain that something white had moved just within the line of trees. He was certain, too, that whatever was white must be Brumby. Of course! That was the answer to his prayers. It was just that the herd had not reached the plain as yet. The half-light played tricks with his eyes; he was passionately sure that the patch of white he had seen was there again.

Encouraging himself and building on what he had seen, he began making his way down the mountain. Joey's satisfaction was short-lived. He found that it would take more than a flash of white seen at sunset on the far side of the plain to convince his father that the herd had returned. Jim did not argue about it, but stated firmly and quietly that Moonlight was to be taken to the Larrakia stallion. Furthermore, he was going himself the next morning to collect the stallion to take it to Bill's.

He looked at his son's troubled eyes and hardened his heart. He spoke slowly, trying to keep the harsh note from his voice.

'You needn't get yourself worked up. Moonlight's not in season yet. The stallion's goin' to be a month or more at Bill's, so I reckon it orter be all right by then. You just get along with your lessons. You'll get used to the idea in a week or two.' He swung himself into the saddle and Joey stood silent, a thin, brown child with very blue eyes

whose small face looked pinched and old in his serious-
ness. Jim turned in his saddle and added,

'I won't get back till tomorrow night – it's too far for
Trixie, an' McMaster'll want the stallion spelled through
the heat of the day. You'd better stay overnight with Mrs
Brett, she'll like to have you. Geoff'll be there, you'll
enjoy that.' Summoning up a smile, he called, 'Good-bye,
son.'

The hot sunlight beat down on Joey's bleached head as
he bent it and looked with puzzled, unseeing eyes at the
dry earth through which his big toe was idly scraping
patterns. Dragging his feet, he went into Moonlight's
stable. Her pale, shining body gleamed in the half-dark-
ness, it was still light enough for Joey to mourn over her
battered head and her one sightless eye as he always did.
She moved with a limp too, not much of a limp, but one
which his father said would never improve. It did not
seem to worry her, when there was rain in the air she
galloped about the paddock and kicked up her heels as
vigorously as any sound mare might have done.

Moonlight had become tame. She allowed Joey to
groom her, to feed her, and to slip on a halter and ride
her bareback as he often rode Flash when they went to
find the sweet pickings that lingered on the mountainside. She had never been broken to saddle and bridle, but
Joey guided her by the balance of his body, the pressure
of his knees, and also by the pressure of the halter-strap
across her nose, which was quite enough to stop her.
Joey had fastened two ends of the halter to this strap
and he could control her with this as he might have done
with a bit. Of course there was no real riding pleasure to
be had from bestriding Moonlight, doing so was simply
expediency; she had no gaits, just a wilful medley of
paces, all of them marred by the halt her lameness gave
her.

Saddest of all for Joey was the fact that while Moonlight made no objection to being cared for and ridden short distances – with rewards at the end of them – she never gave any signs of affection for Joey himself, never never came to his call unless he rattled the feed-bucket, never seemed to care whether it was Joey or Jim who tended her. Joey spent hours rubbing her ears and mourning over that beautiful, tragically marred head, but if Moonlight got tired of it she would nip him severely, as if to say, 'For goodness' sake, leave me alone!'

Yet nothing she could do, no lack of loving response could alter Joey's love for her. His eyes seldom saw the battered body, the marred head of the elegant little mare limping about her pasture. He saw her instead as a graceful beast whose cadenced movements filled him with joy, the way she would have been except for Dugan.

Joey retreated into the cool of the stable, watched Moonlight and brooded on the treachery that had been planned against Brumby. Gradually an idea crept into his mind. His father wouldn't be back until it was dark the next night. Perhaps he could take Moonlight, find Brumby, mate them straight away, and then catch Moonlight, bring her back and be home by the time his father got back. He argued to himself that if he did this his father would really be pleased. It was just that he did not believe that Joey had seen Brumby, whereas Joey knew that he had.

His decision made, Joey stood up. He went to the wall and lifted down his double-reined halter from its nail. He put it on Moonlight and led her outside. If they hurried, they would reach the line of trees through which he had caught his glimpse of Brumby before it got really hot. There was plenty of feed after the rain. Flash would be all right and he had done all his chores. Perhaps his father would be angry that he had missed school, but he would have to chance that. One thing he was quite sure about, Mrs Brett would understand when it was possible for him to explain to her why he had to do this thing.

It was a long, hot ride across the plain over which Joey had so often looked from his vantage point high on the mountainside. Joey noticed that in spite of the rain the great cracks in the red earth seemed bigger than ever and the sides were more treacherously crumbly. He steered Moonlight carefully across or around them. When they reached the trees he slid from Moonlight's back and let her graze as he looked about the ground. Sure enough, there were hoof-marks that were no older than the night before. His heart beat with joy.

When he decided that the mare had rested long enough Joey jumped on to her back again, and followed the swath of trampled earth and broken bushes that showed which way a herd of horses had gone. It never entered Joey's mind to doubt that the makers of the trail were Brumby's herd.

As the day wore on and the trail was less plainly marked, Joey felt very tired. Moonlight's halting gait wearied him twice as much as riding a saddle-broken horse would have done, but the mare herself seemed fresh enough. Joey stuck to it; with every step forward he felt he was getting nearer his goal and any amount of weariness was worth that. He began to feel hungry, and as there was no lack of water, for the creeks and pools were brimming after the rain, he drank a lot and that helped. All the same he wished he had thought to bring some tucker with him.

When darkness descended, and he could no longer see the trail, Joey dismounted and tied Moonlight firmly to a stump. He did not want to lose sight of her until that great moment when he imagined himself slipping the halter from her head and watching her leave him for

Brumby's herd. He never gave any thought to the difficulty he might have in catching her later. He knew nothing of the savage possessiveness felt by every wild stallion for his own mares, nor had he thought that she might not want to return to him. A bush-bred boy of Joey's age would have known all these things and many more, but Joey had not been born in the bush.

Joey broke a stick, and after he had tethered Moonlight he began looking about for a place to sleep. The ground was damp and the leaves he stirred up with his stick were even damper, but that could not be helped. He searched about to make sure that no snakes or other lethal creatures were already there to share his bed and shuddered as his probing stick turned over a piece of bark and a six-inch-long centipede, its body the livid white of a creature of the darkness, crawled away. Finally he collected a little heap of leaves and curled himself up at the foot of a tree, twisting himself into a tight ball, apprehensive of every movement near to him, the rustle of leaves, the faint scratching on the bark of the tree or the soft flutter of wings from some night-flying insect. He was cold, and the night wind blew through his thin, ragged shirt, so he shivered a lot and slept little.

When morning came it was a very drawn-faced, weary-eyed little boy who got up from his uncomfortable couch, and, glad to be moving, undid Moonlight's halter, climbed wearily on to her back and set off once more.

Worry added to Joey's trials. He worried that his father would get home before he could. The thought of the cold, brackish creek water nauseated him, but because he had no food he forced himself to drink a little.

It was a few hours after dawn when he broke through the scrub into an overgrown clearing on the banks of a creek and found the ruins of a selector's old hut, behind which grew a few stunted fruit trees, bearing on their exhausted boughs nobbly pieces of insect-eaten fruit.

Joey picked what fruit he could find. He sat on the ground and sorted it over, and with his nose wrinkling with distaste he bit into it cautiously, shuddering when his teeth narrowly missed a grub or a weevil. He put some of the uneaten fruit inside his shirt and tightened the belt round his thin middle, telling himself that he felt better for this meagre meal.

As he rode on his worry increased. It was getting towards evening. Soon his father would be home, and what would he think? He would probably imagine that Joey was still with the Bretts, and then when he did not come he would ride over there. He would be sure to wonder why the cows had not been rounded up, and what had become of Moonlight; perhaps he would guess and be very angry. Oh, if only he and Moonlight could catch up with Brumby's herd without any more delay!

Hope, that had ridden so buoyantly in Joey's heart, began to sink. Perhaps they would never catch up with the herd. No, he refused to think that way. What would happen, he felt sure, was that Brumby would begin leading his herd back towards the mountain so that they would overtake Moonlight and himself. Possible danger to himself from the great silver stallion never entered Joey's mind.

That night he tried again to sleep on the ground, but he found himself even colder and more sleepless. When morning came his head felt dull, his eyes refused to focus properly and his legs and arms trembled as he tried to drag himself on to Moonlight's back. Once there, he could not see the trail any longer for the flashes of darkness that passed across his sight, so he had to leave the way to Moonlight, who seemed willing enough to forge ahead in the hoof-marks of the wild horses.

Moonlight's dot-and-carry-one gait was probably no more marked, but now Joey found it very hard to stay on her back. His head reeled and he felt deathly sick. He told himself he must be weak from hunger, although he seemed to have no desire at all for food. He burned with thirst, but he was afraid to dismount from Moonlight's back, afraid that he would not be able to mount again in his weak state. His swollen eyes filled with tears and he squeezed them back. He must go on; he never considered doing anything else.

Somehow Joey got through that awful day. From where he rode the trees seemed to sway and to rush around him, and he wondered if the day was really over and the darkness deepening, or if it was just the way he felt that made everything so dark and swaying, himself so giddy?

When he could no longer see at all, Joey slid wearily from Moonlight's back. Something told him that they were beside water and he held on to the halter and lay on his stomach drinking greedily, coughing as his nose dipped beneath the surface, needing desperately to feel the liquid sliding down his burning throat. He heard the sounds of Moonlight beside him, sucking the water through her teeth. Then, her thirst partially satisfied, she chopped her head up and down chewing the water, finally pawing the surface and sending a shower of spray over the boy's burning body.

Painfully he crawled back from the edge of the pool, still clutching the halter-reins. He could not rise to his feet but went on all fours like some wounded animal. Once something alive squirmed from beneath his palm but he was beyond fear. Other small life scuttled or slid through the fallen leaves and he crawled on until he ran head-on into something immovable.

He felt about with his hands, for his eyes could not

help him, and he found he was touching a stump; the butt of a broken bough stuck out a couple of feet from the ground and his fumbling fingers tied the halter to this.

The strain of kneeling and stretching was too much for him. He felt the mounting waves of sick blackness and clutched the stump with both skinny arms, knowing they were sliding down the rough bark, sliding until his body was doubled up and he collapsed into unconsciousness at the foot of the stump.

It was late when Jim Meehan rode up to the hut on tired old Trixie. Usually at this hour Joey had lit the lamp, usually he came running out to meet his father, his face aglow. But tonight no wedge of pale light fell from the doorway to spread across the hard red earth; there was no shout of greeting, no ragged little figure jumping from the door-step to come tearing across to the stable, the hardened soles of his bare feet slapping the earth.

Surely Joey was not sulking over the thought of Moonlight being taken to the Larrakia stallion? That would be so unlike Joey that Jim dismissed the thought as soon as it was born, and he went about bedding down Trixie. As he rubbed her lathered back he saw the dark form of Flash looming up beside him. That was odd; Flash usually grazed about the creek at night. He finished with the mare before it struck him that Moonlight was being very quiet. Not the smallest sound came from her stall. He peered inside the door. It was fairly dark inside the stable, but Moonlight's pale body always shone through the gloom; it did not shine that night because Moonlight was not in her stall. He struck a match and looked around. The halter was gone from its usual place on the wall. Jim's face was very grim as he strode towards the hut.

Inside the hut everything was much as he had left it, but there was no sign of Joey, nothing to indicate where he might be found. His father stood looking around him for a moment. He was tired, and had had a gruelling two days, but whatever Joey was up to, and he more than half suspected what it was, he was going after him, and he was going now. Euro Downs must be his first port of call, for he had delivered the stallion to Bill Regan and Joey had not been with Bill.

He went back to the stable to get his bridle, and hesitated a minute. Trixie was even more tired than he was himself, it seemed unfair to take her out again, so he went after Flash. Flash was fresh, but not at all pleased to have a man's weight on his back after becoming used to Joey's light body.

Jim rode Flash slowly and it was quite dark before he had gone half-way to the Bretts'. He saw Geoff and Rowena lying back in the long 'squatter's' chairs, two shapeless forms on a verandah partially lit through the windows of the living room. He rode up from the creek and shouted when he neared them,

'Hi! This is Jim – have you seen anything of Joey?'

The two dark forms rose from their chairs to the creaking of the canvas, and Geoff called back,

'No, we haven't seen 'im. Rowena says he didn't come to school this mornin' – we thought you musta given 'im somethin' to do at home?'

Jim swung his long leg across Flash's rump and landed on the ground before he answered. He flung the reins over the hitching post and came towards the verandah.

'Joey's gone – an' so has Moonlight.'

Rowena spoke in a puzzled voice.

'But, Jim, why should Joey take Moonlight away?'

'I'm not sure, but I think it's something to do with the stallion I brought from Larrakia to Bill's place today. I told Joey I was goin' to take Moonlight to the stallion when she come on season an' you'd a' thought I was spoilin' hers and his precious Brumby's lives forever, the way he looked at me.'

Geoff gave a short laugh, but Rowena looked worried.

'He's only a little boy,' she said softly, 'a little boy who had no one and nothing of his own until he was six. It's only natural that he clings to you and the horses and everyone around him because that's all his world is composed of, and he's not sure yet if it really *is* his world.'

'Yes, but where's he gone? I don't understand.' Geoff's voice was puzzled now.

'My guess is he's taken Moonlight and gone lookin' for Brumby.'

Geoff whistled. 'My God! I hope he doesn't find 'im – not if he's ridin' Moonlight. That big silver boy's a real killer.'

'I wonder if you'd lend me a horse?' asked Jim. 'Old Trixie's just about all-in and Flash ain't much good for my weight. As soon as it's light I'll be over at the scrub to try and trail the mare.'

'Of course you can take your pick of the horses, and I'm comin' with you. I wish there was somethin' we could do tonight, but it's too dark for trackin'. We'll yard the horses tonight and get off before dawn. Stay here the night, Jim, you don't want to be on your own at a time like this?'

'What if Joey comes back under his own steam?'

'Somehow I'm sure he won't do that. Stay here, we'll ride by the hut on our way out.'

It was more than an hour before dawn that Rowena moved about the kitchen getting breakfast for the two men. She also cut sandwiches for them. She gave Geoff a bandage and one or two simple first-aids and told him to put them in his saddle-bag. The two men rode off into the darkness as the first silvery-green line showed on the eastern horizon.

When they had ridden across the dusty plain and into the scrub it was light enough to see the somewhat stale swath cut by the brumby herd. Overprinted on the massed hoof-marks was the occasional imprint of Moonlight's sharp little hooves, following in the general direction the herd had taken.

They rode as swiftly as they could; in each man's mind was the hideous thought of what might happen to the little boy if he caught up with the brumby herd before they found him.

It was well into the afternoon when they found the bedraggled heap of leaves on which Joey had spent that first night. Later they came on the old fruit trees and even the gnawed, weevily fruit.

'Looks like the kid didn't even have the sense to take some tucker with him,' Jim said.

It was almost noon the next day before they saw the silver body of Moonlight grazing quietly about among the trees. Then they saw the stump and Joey's unconscious figure sprawled beneath it. Jim swung himself down from his horse and picked up the little boy. Joey's breathing was shallow and he had been unconscious for some hours. Geoff and his father looked down at him with anxious eyes, and Geoff said,

'Jim, can you carry the kid all the way? I'll ride back as quickly as I can and get Rowena over to your hut to wait for you with anything she thinks Joey'll need. I'll change horses when I get home and go straight on for the doctor.'

Jim nodded, his throat too tight to speak. He held the light little body with one arm as he mounted and then fastened the end of Moonlight's halter to the cleats on his saddle. He knew he would have to ride slowly, but that way Moonlight would lead all right. Something told him that it was necessary to take Moonlight back home safely, to know where she was when Joey became conscious – 'If Joey becomes conscious,' he said to himself despairingly, his heart full of fear for his boy.

Geoff disappeared into the scrub and Jim could hear the crashing of his horse as he rode him flat out over logs and through the tangled scrub until the sounds of his progress disappeared into the distance.

Jim had a nightmare ride, plodding forward, the reins for the most part on his horse's neck, while Joey mumbled to himself and the fever burned through his wasted body and made his father's arm unbearably hot. Jim kept one hand free to hold out to protect the child whenever a bush or a branch looked like whipping back on to him.

Moonlight led peaceably enough, and the sharp spiciness of the sap-filled bush rose around them, filling the air with its tang, rising from beneath the bruising feet of the horses as they broke the delicate twigs and crushed the fallen leaves. When towards evening Joey became quieter and lay with his body limp and his eyes closed, fear turned in Jim's heart as a knife might have done.

The man was almost exhausted as he rode up to the hut and silently handed his little boy down into Rowena's arms. He saw to his horses in a mechanical way, and when he came inside his forlorn heart was warmed to find the hut spick and span, a meal cooking on the stove and Rowena bending over Joey who was in his own bunk. He lay very white and still while Rowena tried to drop brandy between his tightly clenched teeth.

Jim looked down at his son, his face grey and tired. Rowena straightened up beside him.

'That's about all we can do until the doctor comes.'

Jim still lingered by his boy.

'He's such a little feller,' he said softly, 'but he's got plenty guts to do what he did.'

Rowena turned away from washing her hands in the tin basin and picked up the ragged towel before she said,

'Joey's got more than that, he's got ideas too. He's not just another bush boy. He has dreams and he's willing to pay for them to come true. Sometimes you think Joey's soft; so he is compared with most bush boys, and if I were you I'd be glad of it. When he needs courage he's got plenty.'

The tall woman walked to the fire and set about getting a meal, adding, 'I hope Geoff and the doctor get here soon to help him.'

Part Four: The Homecoming

Brumby, instinct with pride in his new herd, led them northwards while Joey pursued them on his precious Moonlight. They moved steadily away from him. For weeks they walked and grazed farther and farther from the great natural corral where their leader had been born and towards which he was irresistibly drawn every now and again.

Gradually the horses drifted into a country that was more thickly populated; inevitably stockmen scouring the big runs at mustering time caught glimpses of the brumby herd. Once, a man coming from the dark scrub at the foot of a rocky bluff looked upwards and saw the superb form of Brumby, his body burnished to silver by the sunlight, his splendid head held high while the wind whipped his mane and tail into waving fronds that billowed against the intense blue of the sky.

When the stockman returned to the station homestead and spoke of what he had seen, the other men decided they must all organize a brumby run. Each man hoped it might be his luck to rope the silver horse – if he proved to be as fine an animal as he was alleged to be.

The earlier rains followed the herd in their wanderings, heavy storms still hung about and broke over isolated districts. Perhaps it was an age-old instinct that had come down to him from his Arabian forebears that sent Brumby to lead his mares from the softer lowlands up to the hard, stony mountains. To a greater degree than any other breed of horse, the Arab keeps its size and its characteristics. It is slightly affected by changes in feed and water, but its weakness is a tendency towards hoof-ailments. Arabs, reared in the desert on rough, dry ground, are sound of hoof. Transplanted to soft, mushy ground their hooves suffer. So it was that some of Brumby's mares developed hoof-trouble. This soon left them when they followed him up into the hard, well-drained hills.

The brumby run was arranged for a time when heavy storms swept the land and the rivers and creeks were swollen with discoloured floodwaters. Some of the herd had had their eyes affected by fly-carried blight; flies swarmed as the hot, steamy sunshine poured down on the land and the rain ceased for a couple of days.

The Sunday chosen for the run turned out to be one of these hot days. The river winding at the foot of the mountains was, when seen from high up, like a swollen yellow snake as it carried down ochreous mud, and still rose from rains higher up.

The herd moved about the mountains, cropping the pockets of green grass which grew sweeter on the sloping, well-drained ground than they did on the rather sodden lowlands where the brumbies had fed during their wanderings.

Brumby did not know his way about these new ranges as yet. He learned much about the terrain as they wandered in search of feed, and neither man nor anything else had frightened the herd.

Brumby moved serenely about his mares and foals, filling his great belly with the sweet-rooted grass, keeping his mares under control, nipping stragglers and, if that was not enough, keeping order in a very practical way, ruling them with his iron hooves. There were about thirty mares and perhaps a dozen foals, and as the mob was so large they had to spread out more than they did upon the plains, and graze upon several mountain ridges at the same time.

It was the far-off barking of dogs that made Brumby lift his head and sniff the wind. He was not particularly disturbed. It was a long time since his brush with Lugg's savage pack, and the barking of dogs was an often-heard sound which carried little suggestion of an unpleasant aftermath. Nevertheless he trotted about, placing his herd; his mane and tail streamed on the wind behind him, and then, as he turned, blew forward, making a great silver-white wave across his head and his flanks. He dropped his head again to feed and the barking came nearer. With an annoyed shake of the head he trotted to where he could see far out over the plains.

Half a dozen men rode below him, and as many dogs ran just ahead of their horses. As Brumby's head appeared on the cliff-top, one of the men shouted and pointed, then they all spurred their horses and galloped towards the foot of the hill. This forward movement was something of which Brumby did not approve. He turned back and gave the wild, neighing call that he used to alert his herd. Then he began weaving about, getting all the mares and foals welded together so that he could marshal them down the mountainside, away from the dogs and the men below them.

This time the men knew the mountains better than Brumby did. They galloped their horses to where he would expect to descend, and as his wild head appeared, they drove him back up the mountain again.

'Head 'im off! Git 'im on to the river cliff!' a voice shouted. The barking dogs took the lead and rushed up the slope.

Brumby was at a disadvantage both because of his lack of knowledge of the terrain, and also because the spurs of rock, the ledges and small feeding spots tended to split his herd and make it difficult for him to weld them into a single unit. He turned and drove the mares and foals forward. Sure-footed and muscular, it was not difficult for them to put on a good pace even with the disabilities that touched them. A broad ledge along which the stream of horses could gallop led unevenly down the mountainside.

What Brumby did not know was that this same ledge after leading downwards for a time came to an abrupt stop in the face of an unclimbable wall. On the other side a steep cliff fell away to where the swollen river had risen several feet higher than usual up its face.

The brumby runners blocked the way back; they had used this manoeuvre before. The brumbies in the past could not face the twenty-foot plunge into the river; as they charged back the ropes were out and the men waiting to turn the rushing herd, which was usually leaderless, for the stallion, leading down the ledge, was behind the herd when they turned to rush back. The men and the dogs aimed to drive them all into a cliff-edged pocket in which they could be held at will.

Brumby drove his mares along the narrow ledge. It seemed as if a river of horseflesh was flowing before him. The leading mares reached the dead end and turned in panic. A mare and her yearling foal, screaming with terror as only horses can scream, pitched over the steep edge and fell into the river to be carried away on the flood, turning over and over as their water-darkened bodies were borne swiftly away.

The stallion wheeled, rising on his hind legs and neighing his furious challenge. He plunged back to lead the mares away, but before him he saw the men and dogs. He wheeled again and pushed his great body through the packed mares so that several teetered dangerously on the edge. In one place it crumbled, and two more mares fell into the water below. Brumby gave his whistling cry to follow and led the way back, trying once again to find a way out.

The men stopped their horses and called the dogs to heel, waiting at their chosen place, confident of victory. But the dogs were too excited to be controlled. They came rushing and barking towards the herd. Brumby reached the dead-end; again he wheeled, his startled eyes saw the waiting men, the wild-eyed slavering dogs, and with his high neigh he crouched back on his muscular haunches and gave a great bound that sent his body in a splendid arc over the rushing water. Several of the mares tried to follow and the others broke back, fearing the dogs and the men less than the giddy plunge over the cliff.

A shout went up from the men. One of them rode to the cliff's edge and peered downwards, the others turned the mares into the rocky crevice.

Brumby plunged into the rushing water and sank, the plummeting bodies of three of his mares following him. They all sank and the current gripped them. Then the crested neck and narrow intelligent head of the stallion appeared from the water lower down. He swam grandly, his splendid body turned from silver to pewter by the water, his mane and tail spread on the swirling surface, drenched and drawn under or floating like a fleece according to the way the current swept them. He turned his head and saw his mares swimming too, but not even Brumby could swim against the flood to cut across it and reach the shore. It carried him down river and he swam with it, keeping his head above the water, snorting when it got into his nostrils, and breathing deeply when he could keep them clear of the surface.

For three miles the currents swept him along helplessly, but he managed to keep his head up. Then ahead of him a small island divided the rushing water. Once it had been much larger, and the river split and branched around it in two channels. Now it was no more than a mound of mud that would not long remain above water.

It gave Brumby a breathing space. His hooves sank into the soft surface, but he dragged himself out of the water, stood four-square and gave his body a mighty shake. Great drops of water flew from it looking as if part of the silver of which the horse was composed had become free as it was flung from his water-darkened body in a cloud of spray.

As he looked across the water he saw the heads of the three mares bobbing on the current and he neighed shrilly. Two of the mares reached the island and dragged themselves from the water, but the third mare was too exhausted, and her dark body swept past, bobbing and turning in the swirling water.

The three horses lifted their hooves nervously up and down in the soft mud. They bent their heads and sniffed it, and one of the mares gave the tremulous whinny that means danger. They were both nervous of the knob of muddy earth that gave them such a precarious foot-hold, but reassured by the great bulk of the stallion in whom they were used to placing their trust. They needed the rest, the respite from the tugging and pulling of the water and the strain of keeping their heads above the surface. Gradually the heaving of their sides quietened down.

The water was rising, and their hooves clung to the softened mud beneath them as it came implacably higher and higher. The shore receded and Brumby moved rest-lessly, nostrils distended, his wide-open eyes on the river that rushed downwards in ever-changing deep yellow folds that had none of the thin transparency of water, but moved more like heavy, sluggish yellow oil, opaque and appearing almost solid.

Presently the stallion's movements became jerkier; the water was above his knees, rising fast, and his hooves pressed into the treacherous softness. He seemed to make up his mind. Shaking his head he turned in the water so that he faced downstream, and stood behind one of the frightened mares. With little plunges, deadened by both flood and mud, he nudged at her, whinnying a little, urging her forward into the water; she tried to push backwards in her fear. Brumby's head shot out, his teeth met on her rump, and with a despairing whicker she plunged into the water and was swept downstream.

He turned to the other mare, and when she resisted he moved her impatiently with his shoulder. She too was swept away into the swift-flowing channel pouring downwards. Then, with a snort, the silver horse sprang into the water and swam valiantly after his wives, gaining on them. He reached the mares before the river took a curve around what had once been a ten-foot cliff, but which was now level with the water.

With great plunges Brumby forced the mares across the current until presently they neared the far bank and were able to climb from the water, snorting and trembling, shaking themselves and stamping their hooves as if they could not believe they really stood on solid land once again.

When all the shaking and stamping was over, Brumby drove them into the scrub that bordered the river. He kept them moving until they reached higher land. It was wild and deserted and they settled down to graze.

The impassable river lay between the horses and their pursuers. From a total herd of more than forty mares and foals, two mares and the stallion alone remained together.

So Brumby found himself back where he had been almost a year before, lord of an insignificant herd. But the drift back soon began. The wild stallion's acquisitiveness paid off in the capture of three more mares, one with a yearling foal, and with this small harem he roamed the bush drifting imperceptibly, always a little nearer to his own mountain. Perhaps the brumby run that proved so disastrous for the herd was the thing that turned his instinctive memory towards the place of his birth, the high mountain corral which had been his home and his place of safety for the first year of his life.

The storms and floods had spent themselves, the lush, soft land of the plains dried up, the soil hardened and the grass became sparser and sweeter. The rumps of the mares, plentifully marked by the stallion's teeth, testified to the smallness of his ménage. He seemed to be restless and worried most of the time, determined to keep his tiny herd from straying. Often, for no more reason than some inexplicable sound brought to him on the wind, Brumby would lift his head, leave his grazing and begin his swift, long-legged trot, weaving in and out between the mares and finally circling them, rather in the way a figure skater moves over the ice.

Vibrations from the unhurried galloping of several horses sent the stallion arching his neck and rounding up his wives. They were grazing just beyond a piece of scrub-land. Brumby stationed them where he could stand between them and whatever it was that advanced through the scrub. He heard hooves crashing along the littered ground. Presently four mares came out of the scrub at the run. Something had startled them, but as they saw the waiting form of Brumby they broke and tried to scatter around him. He threw up his great head and whistled excitedly, plunging right and left to stop them, so that the mares wheeled, propped and slowed down.

Brumby herded them with excited neighings and whinnyings; they were a remnant of his own herd that escaped the stockmen when Brumby and his two mares plunged into the flooded river. They wandered about the bush looking for a lord, and now they had found him. Once the first excitement passed, the whistling and trotting and snorting, they joined the other mares and followed their former lord. Brumby's herd was growing once more.

Sometimes accident depleted his growing herd, but it was seldom that he lost more than one mare at a time, he was too vigilant for that. Even with his unceasing care disaster occasionally fell upon one of the mares, as when, thirsty after a waterless day, the herd crowded down to a small, sandy-bedded creek. One of the mares, watering a few yards away from the others, having drunk her fill and wishing to return, found her hooves held in a quicksand. The more she struggled, whinnying her fear, the deeper she sank.

Brumby came at her first call. Some instinct, or perhaps an earlier and happier experience, made him circle the dangerous patch. Sometimes he stood and pawed the earth, stretching his crested neck as if he would comfort the unfortunate creature by the touch of his nose. One of his hooves was sucked down, but because the other three were planted on solid ground he managed to pull it out.

Distractedly the stallion wheeled and drove the rest of his herd together, returning again and again to the doomed creature in the quicksand. With torturing slowness the exhausted mare sank lower and lower, only the convulsive movements along her back and sides showed how she still strove to lift her hooves from the deadly grip. Then she seemed to lose heart for the fight, her tired head sank down, gradually she could no longer lift it above the treacherous sand. She died of exhaustion and despair and of the slow breathing of the wet sand that clogged her nostrils.

Still Brumby moved anxiously about her long after nightfall, although there was nothing to see except a long dark blur in the middle of the terrible sand. Before dawn he wheeled away from the place and led his mares back to grass.

A chase by three stockmen riding homewards lost him another mare. The men sighted the brumby herd, and went after it with shouts and cracks of their whips. Through the scrub the wild horses raced with the men after them. But the men's horses had already done a day's work and they soon tired, so the riders turned and went on homewards.

The startled mares continued to gallop with Brumby at their rear, as is the stallion's way when danger comes from behind. The leading mares came up against a wire fence, and all but one swerved to go round it. The one mare tried to jump it and her legs tangled in the barbed wire as she fell heavily to the ground, thrashing and kicking, driving the barbs into her hide, struggling, tearing ugly wounds in legs and shoulders.

Brumby gave his whistling call and the herd slowed up. He went to where he could hear the frightened calling of the mare. With his great hooves he stamped on the wire, pulling a torn strand so taut that the barbs were against the mare's flesh and she began to struggle anew. She freed her near front leg and tried to stand.

Brumby neighed his fury at this thing that was defying him. He reared and brought a striking forehoof down on an unbroken wire. It snapped and the lashing end drove into his leg to the depth of an inch so that he reared and squealed with rage.

Then the mare pulled her trembling body free of the

wire and stood dripping with blood and sweat, her head hanging, flanks heaving, on the wrong side of the fence from the rest of the herd. Angrily Brumby neighed at her, demanding her return, but she would not face the wire again nor would his intelligence let him put his hooves among the wicked stuff. From behind him one of herd neighed urgently and he trotted back to his other mares.

For two days Brumby led the herd on one side of the wire fence and the injured mare followed on the other, seeking to join them once more. Then the mare's wounds became infected. With the fever that was destroying her, her weakness increased. Her last feeble steps led her away from the wire until she lay down beneath a tree and died there.

Brumby was no stranger to death. It is a part of every day to the creatures of the wild, and those who are left waste little time or tears over it. The next day the horses left the fence and plunged back into the wilderness once more.

When at last the doctor came to Joey, the crisis was almost over. It was a very thin, pitifully weak little boy who became for the first time conscious of his father's presence, and at the same time came to an awareness of the last thing he remembered, Moonlight amid the unknown bush around him.

Jim, sitting beside him, longed for a conscious look from his son. He saw the change in the tired blue eyes that opened and looked at him, saw too, with an awareness that had not belonged to him before these long days and nights of vigil over the sick boy, that the gaze turned to one of apprehension. He put his brown hand on the bony little shoulder and looked gravely back at the boy.

'It's all right, son. You've been ill, but now you're going to be well again.'

'Moonlight?' Joey's lips formed the name rather than said it. Jim smiled at him.

'Moonlight's fine. She's out in the stable waiting for you to get better, and she's waiting for Brumby, too. You go to sleep, I'll be here when you wake.'

Joey moved his hand slightly, a hand that was more like the claw of a young bird, and Jim put his own hand over it while Joey shut his eyes and went into a sound sleep.

The days of Joey's convalescence were delightful to him. The child, who had had no real mothering to remember, thrived in the combined loves of his father, of Rowena and Geoff, and of Bill Regan who was a constant visitor. One or the other was always with him.

His father talked to him and even told him stories of the bush; Rowena read to him; Geoff joked with him, and Bill brought along a box which proved to hold hundreds of strips of leather. With these he plaited Joey a bridle of his very own. Joey watched it grow from a few loose strands of leather into the finished article, complete with nickel rings and a light bit that would be kind to Flash's mouth.

'The only trouble with these fancy bridles is that they're not much good on a pullin' horse,' Bill told him. He held up a rein and ran his finger down the serrated edge. 'You don't want to get that edge jerked through your hand or you're likely to miss a strip o' skin.'

'Flash'll like it,' Joey said. 'He never pulls much.'

Bill shook his head wisely. 'Yer never know. Flash'll be fresh as paint when you begin ridin' 'im again.'

Joey smiled smugly, he liked to pretend that Flash was a very dashing steed.

Gradually Joey's convalescence ended and he took up

his old life again, doing his chores, caring for Moonlight and Flash, riding to have lessons from Rowena. Almost every day he rode up the mountain, climbed to his lookout, and gazed hungrily across the plain. His belief remained unshaken; some day the brumby herd, led by the fierce great stallion, would leave the scrub, cross the plains and climb the mountain to settle in the great natural corral that had been the birth-place of the leader.

One evening, as he lay on his stomach peering over the plain with its dark gullies, its dust hazy red in the setting sun, he was certain that once again something that appeared to have no more substance in it than a white shadow moved within the edge of the scrub. It was Brumby, Joey was certain it was Brumby.

This time he knew that he must not take Moonlight and go and see for himself; he had promised his father that he would never do that again. He scrambled down from his perch, and beating a tattoo with his sharp bare heels on the astonished Flash's ribs, he rode home and told his father. Jim nodded his head.

'If the herd's as near as all that, one day they'll find their way up the mountain, you can be sure of that.'

Joey spent more time than ever in his eyrie. He did most of the work about the place now, for work for his father was plentiful a few miles away, and Jim went off every day.

'We'll have enough money for fences some day, if this keeps up, Joey. Then when your herd's back we can really keep them in and start to breed.'

Joey beamed. It seemed to him that now his father really did understand, and perhaps he did. Jim's mind often went back to Rowena's words when Joey was ill. He tried to sympathize with his son's single-mindedness; a new gentleness and understanding had grown from the little boy's weakness, and his long fight to get well again.

Joey watched the scrub and the plain so consistently that at last even his father ceased to doubt that the herd was drifting back again, and then one night Joey wakened. It seemed to him that outside in the moonlight something jarred the ground, and that after that some stealthy movement was going on outside. He slipped out of his bunk and went to the window just as a soft whickering noise came to his ears.

At first he saw nothing. Then from around the corner of the stable he saw something that made him catch his breath. With the great crest of his neck arched, his body frosted by moonlight, tense, nervous, blotting out the dingy slabs that made the wall of the stable, Brumby moved like a luminous shadow, alert, distressed by the nearness of man, yet unable to resist the lure of the mare in season. The stallion whickered softly and was answered from inside the stable by Moonlight.

Joey felt rather than saw his father come to his side, and together they peered out into the ghostly night.

'I'm glad Flash is down by the creek,' Joey whispered.

'And Trixie too,' Jim whispered back. 'That silver devil'll make off with Trixie if I don't watch out.'

'I wish we could let Moonlight out of the stable?'

Jim looked down at the child. 'Don't ever try to do that. If Brumby saw anyone moving he'd be sure to rush him, then I'd have to shoot your horse.'

Silently they watched the ghostly, yet mighty body moving about the stable.

'He's beautiful – and he's mine!' Joey said proudly, glancing round at the shelf on which the tin box stood, holding the precious bill of sale which made him the owner of this great creature.

'Couldn't we leave Moonlight out tomorrow night?'

'I'd rather not. Of course she's your mare, an' you can decide. But I believe it'd be better to wait a little. The horses'll drift back to the mountain, I'm sure of it, and when they do you'll have a chance of getting Moonlight back. If you let her go with Brumby now she'll be off to the scrub, perhaps for good if anything should frighten the herd, then you'll never have a foal of Moonlight's and Brumby's. No, son, you've waited so long, wait a little longer, it'll be worth it.'

For an hour the wild horse whinnied and pawed, bit and stamped, and Moonlight answered him. Towards dawn he wheeled and trotted proudly back the way he had come.

Jim knew that the wild horse would return but that it would always be through the night, and then only for as long as Moonlight remained in season. He made Joey promise to be home by dark and to stay in the hut after that. As an extra precaution Flash and Trixie were both tethered on Geoff's side of the creek.

Joey went to his look-out in the afternoons and he was often rewarded by the sight of wild bodies moving, the occasional flash of white, in the fringe of the scrub opposite. He willed the wild horses to come back to the mountain; lying on his stomach he would close his eyes and count fifty very slowly, telling himself that when he opened his eyes he would see Brumby coming out of the scrub followed by the herd, all ready to begin their return to the mountain. But the horses remained obstinately where they were, and sometimes Joey even became discouraged and wondered if they might not go away, return northwards as they had before. Yet he never quite lost heart.

'What's the matter, Joey?' Rowena asked him one day as he sat at the table on the shady, vine-covered side of the veranda where he had his lessons. Joey had developed

very much in the months since his illness. He took the
end of the pencil from his mouth and tried to pull himself together as he answered,

'It's Brumby. Dad says he will come back to the mountain, so why doesn't he come?'

It was not long after this that Dugan appeared about
the district again. Time had not dealt kindly with him;
his face was older and meaner. The truth was that he
had suffered with intermittent pain in his head ever since
he was thrown by Brumby. His hatred of the wild horse
increased with the months. He wanted to capture him,
to starve and beat him into submission – and at the same
time he toyed with the idea of shooting the stallion as he
had shot Yarraman. Such a death was too easy from
Dugan's point of view, and so when he heard that the
brumbies were back in the district he made long-term
plans.

It was half an hour before sunset, the time when
Joey sat on the doorstep and played with his latest lizard.
This one was a little fellow whose body was almost
transparently pink from its infancy, and whose toes
seemed knobbly and large in the way of most baby
creatures. Joey loved lizards, they made up for his not
having a dog of his own. He had never asked Jim for a
pup, but only because he knew that it would have to
feed itself, and so he would have to watch it chase
rabbits and kangaroo rats and kill them, and he knew
that he would hate that. When they were rich he would
have lots of dogs because then there would always be
bought feed for them, and there would be no need for
them ever to have to kill anything.

Joey looked up and saw a slouching figure coming
round the end of the stable. It looked like that man
Dugan, but of course it couldn't be, not after what his

father had said to Dugan the day they fought. All the same Joey wished his father was at home. He stood up and put his lizard down carefully. It *was* Dugan. Joey was not sure what he ought to say. When Dugan called out,

'Hello, kid!'

Joey replied with a not very cordial,

'Hello.'

Dugan looked down at the box with the small lizard in it and said,

'Thought you'd a' been playin' with dolls.'

Joey's brown face flushed and he made no answer. Dugan placed himself on the step, picking a stem of the dry grass that grew patchily about the door, and asked in an innocent voice,

'Where's yer dad?'

'At work. He'll be back soon.' Joey rubbed the sole of one bare foot on his other instep. Dugan laughed.

'It don't matter, you'll do as well. 'Ow's that mare yer got th' day of th' brumby run?'

'Moonlight's all right,' Joey said stiffly. His face went red with suppressed anger that Dugan, who had so grievously injured the mare, should dare to ask about her.

'I'm after the big white stallion,' Dugan went on. 'They tell me 'e comes around after th' mare?'

Joey thought quickly. His father had told Dugan that he would have no more brumby running on his property; but Brumby's herd was not on the property, it was just across the boundary marked by the scrub. He was silent, not knowing what to say. Then he decided desperately to play what he believed was his trump card.

'You can't touch Brumby, Mr Rutland sold 'im to Dad to give to me on my birthday,' he began breathlessly.

Dugan leaned back on his elbow, chewed on the grass stem and looked at Joey with hard, cynical eyes.

'Is that so?' he asked sarcastically. 'Well, that's too bad, that stallion's a brumby an' 'e belongs to anyone 'oo can catch 'im.'

Joey, thoroughly agitated, brushed past Dugan and ran to the shelf that held his box enclosing the precious bill of sale. With trembling fingers he opened the box and took out the piece of paper, holding it out to Dugan.

'Look, it says there that Brumby's my horse! That's the bill of sale Mr Rutland gave my dad.'

Dugan raised a lazy hand and pulled the paper out of Joey's fist, saying,

'Yer'll need more'n that kid stuff ter stop me! You don't own no 'orse.'

Trembling with rage and fear Joey stooped down to retrieve the paper that Dugan had thrown contemptuously on to the floor. Dugan reached out and caught his ankle so that the little boy fell on the floor.

'Don't you git fresh with me, kid. I come 'ere to tell your dad I'm willin' ter pay fer runnin' th' brumbies, an' 'e can 'ave 'is pick when we done it – except fer the stallion, 'e's mine.'

Joey picked himself up in a passion of rage.

'My dad told you you can't run brumbies on our place!'

Dugan laughed and spat.

'I'll run 'em where I like – they don't stay on th' mountain night and day, yer know.'

Through his rage Joey registered that Dugan didn't know that the herd had still not returned to the mountain, that they were always on land where he was free to run them as much as he liked.

Joey remembered the slaughter of Yarraman, he thought of the mutilation of Moonlight's beautiful head, he looked at the stupid, ill-natured face of the man on the step, the slight but grotesque twisting of his heavy shoulder that gave him such a sinister look, and his passion of rage and fear made him cry shrilly,

'You get out of here! You're a bully an' you're cruel too. This place belongs to my dad an' me an' we don't want you! You get out —or my dad'll be home an' give you a hidin' like 'e did before!'

'Keep yer 'air on, you – kid – I'm goin', I don't wanter see yer dad now, I know wot I wanter know. If 'e come 'ere now we'd see 'oo'd git th' 'idin' – 'ittin' me when I wasn't lookin'!'

'That's a lie! It's a lie! You get out!' Joey rushed past Dugan and ran to where he could look down the slope of the hill, while he called frantically, 'Dad! Dad!'

From down near the creek came an answering shout. Joey's relief was boundless. He turned and ran back towards the hut. There was no sign of Dugan. Joey guessed he must have walked into the bush on the other side of the hut, but he didn't care now, he was only relieved that the man had gone away.

Jim, riding home on tired old Trixie, heard his son's shouts. He hurried the mare along and saw Joey's ragged little figure flying down the hill. The rage and fear left Joey and his reaction from it made him want to cry, but he wouldn't do that, his father thought that tears were soft, unless you really couldn't help them. He bit back his tears and when he reached his father's stirrup he looked up into his face and forced himself to be calm.

'It was that Dugan, he came wanting to see you. I – I thought he might hurt Moonlight.'

Joey wanted desperately to tell his father how Dugan had said he was going to have another brumby run to catch Brumby, but somehow he couldn't. Perhaps his father would find Dugan and fight him again, and although of course his father would win, that thought did frighten Joey.

When it was full moon Joey always slept more lightly. Sometimes in the morning he found the prints of Brumby's big hooves where he had moved about the stable that held Moonlight, but he had never seen the stallion since that first night.

Joey woke one night of the full moon, feeling sure that he heard Brumby moving quietly about outside. He crept out of bed and went to the window, not wanting to wake his father who had been dog-tired the night before after a long spell of very hard work.

Joey crept to the window and looked out. The moonlight lay in a blaze of white light that showed everything as clearly as if it had been day, except that it shone with its cold, eerie bleakness. Nothing moved, the yard about the stable was deserted. All the same Joey felt little prickings of doubt. He knew inwardly that all was not well.

The boy waited by the window; after five minutes there was still no movement outside. He hesitated. He was worried and wanted to see if Moonlight was all right, but he knew that his father would be angry if he went to the stable during the night. He waited miserably, trying to make up his mind, then his anxiety won. Like a small shadow he slipped quietly out of the door, and keeping an alert watch for Brumby he ran silently to the stable door to peer inside and reassure himself.

Very quietly he lifted the latch of the heavy door. It gave a faint creak and swung inwards. Joey peered into the interior where the white blaze of the moon shone through the wide cracks, making the stable hazy with light. Moonlight was not there. Joey's heart thumped as he peered about in bewilderment, unable to explain how Moonlight could have disappeared and still left the door closed as he had found it. Of course the wind might have blown it to, but the wind would not have moved the latch. Where was Moonlight?

Joey hesitated. He knew that he should wake his father, but knowing how desperately tired he had been the evening before he did not want to disturb him. It was a hot, white night, and Joey ran a little way across the earth to where the hillside began to slope away, and gazed across the land. He could see Flash and Trixie grazing but there was no sign of Moonlight. Perhaps she had broken out of the stable – perhaps she was out when his father took his nightly look around, perhaps he had found the latch up and without looking into the stable he had dropped it down again. Yes, that must have been what happened. If that was so then perhaps Moonlight was on her way to Brumby?

The boy felt he must know, must find out what had really happened. If Moonlight was on her way to Brumby then she would have gone down the hill and across the red, seamed plain that led to the scrub where the brumbies lurked. He decided he couldn't go back to bed, he couldn't sleep until he knew what had happened to Moonlight. He made up his mind, and began running down the hill towards Flash. If Moonlight was on her way to the herd he just might be in time to see her crossing the plain if he hurried to his look-out.

Drumming his heels impatiently on Flash's well-fed sides, he started off to cross the creek on his way to ride up the first quarter-mile of the steep mountain slope. After that Flash could graze and he would climb the rest of the way on foot, for his soles were as hardened as any monkey's.

At last he reached his vantage point and stood, a lonely, ragged little figure silvered by the moonlight, peering out over the plain. His heart leaped. About in the centre of the plain a man was riding; the blazing silver light shone back in a sinister straight line from the rifle he carried across his saddle and from the graceful silver body of the mare he was attempting to lead.

'Moonlight! The man must be Dugan,' Joey thought to himself. 'What did that brute want with Moonlight – hadn't he hurt her enough already? The gun – why should he want a gun?'

Joey could not bear to think what the gun, the mare and the direction Dugan was taking added up to. This was no brumby run, runners were an organized team of horsemen. He stood twisting his hot, sweaty little hands together, a thousand thoughts churning through his mind.

He looked past the man whose horse was struggling to cope with Moonlight. She was trying to pull away, snorting with fear of the rider. Beyond her he could see the movement of big bodies within the rim of the scrub, as he had seen them so often before.

Moonlight lurched violently away, the gun barrel swung up in the air and Dugan came half off his saddle. Joey had not the slightest doubt it was Dugan, even if he had been unable to recognize the man's heavy outline, and he knew that Dugan was using Moonlight as a bait with which to destroy Brumby.

Dugan jerked hard at the lead; Moonlight reared up, and her scream echoed through the thin night air. Dugan dismounted, flung his reins over his shoulder and pulled the stockwhip from the front of his saddle. Joey felt sick, but he could not look away, it seemed as if every tremor of fear, every violent rebellious movement the mare gave was repeated in his own skinny body.

Dugan laid the gun on the edge of the deepest of the big dry cracks that seamed the face of the plain, and then he walked back a few steps. He jerked the lead viciously but Moonlight was full of fight. She screamed again, a high, pained sound, and reared back, flailing her delicate, beautiful legs. Dugan brought the whip-lash crashing across her ribs so that she reared and plunged even more wildly, unable to get away from the man and his horse, to which she was tied.

Even in the pain and horror Joey felt as he watched Dugan, he became conscious of something happening in the speckled shadow of the scrub. Again Moonlight screamed, and out of the scrub poured a flood of horses led by the stallion. The man, intent on the punishment he was giving the mare, heard too late the pounding of hooves, and felt the jarring of the earth as thirty or more horses galloped straight towards him.

With incredible speed the brumbies were on top of him, looking like a long, thin brown wave with its curling silver crest rushing before it. As the man stooped for his gun Brumby reached the far side of the fissure. In one great leap he was across it; he wheeled, and as Dugan tried desperately to escape, to dodge away from this silver demon, the lethal fore-hooves of the horse struck him down and his body toppled into the fissure, while the long line of the herd, the mares and the foals came straight on after their leader. The crumbling dry edges broke under their hooves. They made no attempt to leap across but plunged down into the opening, pounding the body of the man into the earth with their hooves, snorting with fear as they felt the yielding body beneath them instead of earth, snorting and struggling with fright and churning the dry earth into a whirlpool of red dust.

Joey put his hands across his eyes; he could not look any more. He stood with his shoulders hunched in horror, his fingers pressing on his eyes. He did not see the terrified plunging of Dugan's horse as it struggled with Moonlight when the brown, white-flecked flood broke around them.

The stallion wheeled and circled and the mares followed him. Half mad with excitement he turned and galloped straight back, and the mares and foals followed, back over the already pounded fissure, filling it with the dry, red earth, their hooves obliterating any trace of the man or of his gun.

Anyone looking casually at the plain and its wide cracks the next day would see nothing, except that a herd of horses had galloped over one of the great dusty rents in the earth, breaking down the edges, filling it with powdered dust. In the loneliness surrounding it, it might be months before anyone rode that way.

The excitement and the killing of the man had left no room in the stallion's savage heart for either the mare or for Dugan's horse to which she was tethered. Instinctively the mare fought to get away; just as instinctively the saddled and bridled horse braced its legs and fought back to hold her. It had been full of terror at the racing, pounding flood of horses, and then only the struggling of the mare had prevented its running away. It was still frightened, but it fought on stubbornly and would not follow her.

When Joey lifted his hands away from his eyes his narrow body was bathed in sweat and he shook with shock and fear. He saw the last of the mares disappearing into the fringe of the scrub, heard the faint, sharp cracks of trampled sticks beneath the many hooves and guessed that the wild herd was already running, running away once more from the mountain.

On the plain below him he saw the struggling horses. Like a wound the big, earthy crack lay, its centre dark and mysterious, its broken rims edged with reflected light; there was no visible sign of Dugan. Even the sinister gleaming barrel of his gun had been trodden beneath a covering of earth. With it, Joey knew, lay the battered body of the man.

What could he do? His father – of course he must tell his father. But if he did, wouldn't his father have to tell the police that Brumby had killed Dugan? If he did that, then they would hunt Brumby down and shoot him.

Torn with misery, Joey sat on a rock and tried to think clearly. The terrible danger to Brumby, his Brumby was always paramount in his mind; his one clear thought was that he must protect the horse. He told himself that he was right to protect Brumby. Brumby had known nothing except that the man was attacking Moonlight. The gun – surely Brumby was justified in defending his own life, and certainly that gun meant that Dugan was on his way to shoot Brumby.

Head on hands, Joey thought and thought. He could not feel much about Dugan; before his eyes was always Moonlight's scarred head. Dugan had been a brute; for Brumby it was kill or be killed. Whatever was he to do?

His whole body trembled with the urgency of his need to make a decision. At one moment he felt he must tell his father what Brumby had done – the next moment he knew that he couldn't, couldn't doom Brumby to be shot. He looked down at the plain. Moonlight was still wrestling, trying to pull away from the halter. Dugan's heavier horse was being dragged along a few feet at a time, but already they had come half-way to the foot of the steep mountainside where Joey crouched in his misery.

He made up his mind, the biggest problem must wait. First he must get Moonlight again. He needed decision, needed action. He began scrambling down the rocky earth, then paused to pin-point the two struggling horses. He ran the last twenty yards and found himself on the plain. He went as fast as he could across the dry plain, but it took him more than a quarter of an hour of running and gasping, a fierce pain pulsing through his side, before he slowed up so as not to add to the confusion of the two horses.

He stood quite still and began talking to Moonlight. At first she took no notice of his voice as she pulled and tugged, reared and twisted, her body streaked with sweat, her head shaking furiously in an effort to throw off the halter, and the tired brown horse fought her all the time. Sometimes the strength of the slender little mare almost jerked the horse off his feet, but he was a stubborn brute and he dug in his hooves and resisted her.

Gradually Joey's voice seemed to penetrate her brain and her struggles lessened. He went to her and stood quietly beside her, stroking and fondling her. She was drenched in sweat but the terror died away at the touch of his familiar hands, the sound of his voice. Never had she suffered the slightest cruelty at his hands, and though she showed no affection, she trusted the boy.

After a time Joey left the mare. She was quiet now except for her heaving sides and distended nostrils. Joey went to Dugan's horse and put his hand on to the frightened beast's neck. It jerked its head away and Joey's face darkened, he knew what that sudden, frightened movement meant.

'He can never hit you again, old horse,' he said softly, and went on talking: 'I'm sorry I've got to leave you wearing the saddle and bridle, but someone'll find you. I'll have to take you home and chase you the other way because you'll be too frightened to go away by yourself. Come on, let me take the lead off the saddle . . . now then, give me the reins. I'm goin' to ride Moonlight and lead you. After all this she'll never lead, but you will. Come on, we're ready.'

Joey's heart was heavy and his mind was still unable to decide what to do. He knew well enough what he *should* do – tell his father – but what would they do to Brumby then?

He was desperately tired, worn out emotionally and physically, so he climbed gratefully on to Moonlight's back and turned her head towards home while he led the brown horse. He rode around the foot of the mountain and hitched the two horses while he collected Flash and took him, too, across the creek before he left him. He approached the stable from the far side, praying his father would not hear him, put Moonlight into her stable and closed the door.

Then he climbed wearily into Dugan's saddle and rode his unwilling horse for half a mile towards Conway's Gap. He dismounted, picked up a small stick and drove the horse before him until at last it trotted off into the bush.

Utterly weary he turned back, but when he reached home he still had to rub Moonlight down. It wouldn't do for his father to find her caked with sweat, and Joey hoped he would not go near enough to her for a day or two to see the ugly weal raised by Dugan's lash on her side.

It only lacked a couple of hours to dawn when he crept back into the hut. The clock still ticked away and a slanting ray of moonlight told him that he had not been away for much more than three hours. It seemed hard to believe that so many terrible things could happen in so little time. Shivering with weariness the little boy climbed into his bunk, looking across at where his father still slept heavily. Then all worries and problems passed from his brain as he fell into a deep exhausted sleep himself.

Jim looked sharply at Joey's small tired face in the

morning. Since his illness he had formed the habit of watching the boy and that morning he was worried at what he saw.

'You all right, Joey?' he asked.

Joey nodded and later his father rode off rather unhappily while Joey went on with his chores, glad that his father had wakened late and had hurried away leaving some of his usual jobs undone. He had been afraid that his father's sharp eyes would find some telltale evidence of the night's happenings. As they sat down to their mugs of breakfast tea, Joey had an almost overpowering urge to tell his father all about the night, but it passed, and once that moment was over it became doubly difficult for him to contemplate telling him anything about it.

Joey went about his work dully conscious that he had a decision to make, but not feeling up to it. When he finished his work he went for Flash to ride over to the Bretts' for his lessons. He felt listless and very miserable, but he thought if he failed to turn up someone might ask questions. He was trying very hard to hide his terrible secret until at least Brumby and his herd would have gone very far away. He guessed they would roam the distant country probably for some months to come. Then he shivered a little as a cold shudder ran across his thin body at the thought that as they had gone away, so would they return, at least as far as the scrub which they seemed to regard as their home.

He put the bridle on Flash and then for a moment he put his thin arms around the old horse's neck and was comforted by the warmth, the clean sweaty tang that lingered on the hide of his old friend. Then, heavy eyed and heavy hearted, he rode slowly down the hill.

Jim was worried by the change he saw in Joey and he spoke to Rowena about it. She told him what she thought, but she could not help him any further, and because he was overworked, and worried about the little boy, Jim became irritable with him. Joey's heart was lonelier than ever as he felt that his father was drifting away from him.

Joey knew well enough what he should do, but he could not bring himself to do it. He felt that to speak of what he had seen was tantamount to passing a death sentence on the loved stallion. His conscience worried him so much that he would wake through the night, his body bathed in cold sweat, his mind full of terrible imaginings. He tortured himself by thinking that as he was deliberately doing wrong, God would punish him through someone he loved. Perhaps Flash or Moonlight would die – perhaps something would happen to his father? He kept this thought to the last, this most awful thought, and drove it to the back of his mind. But sometimes, when the night was dark and long and the immeasurably sad chorus of the dingoes came to his ears, the conviction grew that he would be punished for doing wrong, and that the punishment would mean the loss of his father's love, or that some terrible physical happening would take Jim from him.

These thoughts were almost beyond bearing. Joey sat on his bunk, wide eyed, the thumping of his heart shaking his thin body, and listened for Jim's breathing; in his fear and distress he told himself that the thing he feared might have happened already.

Rowena sat on her veranda and her long, brown face was filled with sadness. That morning it had been impossible to teach Joey anything, he just wasn't there; he seemed to be listening for something he dreaded; he was a small ghost with a stricken face whose mental misery and sense of wrongdoing was killing him. She sat in an old rocking chair, moving gently; the long, peaceful squatter's chairs were out of tune with her mood.

The sad afternoon sunlight fell across the land. It was dark and comparatively cool on the veranda, shaded by its thick growth of passion vine. She rose, determined to go indoors to get some mending, for something to do with her big brown hands. Anything was better than sitting idle and thinking of Joey's suffering little face.

She glanced through the gap in the vines that framed the four low steps leading up to the veranda. Far on the hillside she saw a small figure on an old horse and she prayed that the moment was drawing near when Joey would confide in her. She forced herself to go into the house and to collect her mending, then she returned to her veranda chair.

Rowena was sitting there, her head bent over her sewing, when Joey came up the steps, dragging his feet, a miserable, frightened look in his eyes. Rowena looked up and gave him the warm smile that was for him alone, the smile that changed every line in her austere tanned face.

'Why, Joey! I am glad you've come, I was feeling lonely. Come and sit with me.'

Joey didn't answer. He perched himself on the wooden edge of a big canvas chair from which his toes barely reached the floor, and he looked at Rowena despairingly. She pretended not to notice, bit the end of a piece of thread and put her sewing basket on the floor beside her, saying,

'I'll get us tea.'

In an instant Joey had flung himself into her lap, his stringy little arms wound tightly round her neck, his small face drenched in tears. Rowena said nothing. She held him to her and let him cry until he was ready to sit up on her knees, his blue eyes wet. He sniffed vigorously and she knew that he wanted to tell her all about it.

Rowena listened gravely and without interruption. When Joey finished she realized how much it had cost him to tell her something that he firmly believed might mean the death of Brumby. She realized as she never had before how much he loved and trusted her, and her own heart was full of love and gratitude.

When he was quiet she smoothed his bleached hair back from his hot forehead and said gently,

'Of course it was wrong not to tell your father at once, but when you do I think you'll find that he'll understand. You've been unhappy about doing wrong, and so, in a way, you've punished yourself. Anyway, you're a man, you can take punishment if your father thinks you should have it.'

Joey nodded. 'It doesn't matter what Dad does to me, it's – it's Brumby –' His voice trailed away. He leaned back against Rowena's shoulder and she went on rocking and holding him closely while she talked.

'Now, you must stop imagining things. I don't know what your father'll decide to do, but I do know one thing, he'd never punish a dumb brute because it doesn't know the difference between right and wrong. Whatever he decides you may be sure it will be the kindest thing in the end for Brumby. You must stop worrying, there are plenty of people to share things with you now. Joey, remember that nothing is ever as bad as it seems when you're lying awake in the night, or when you've thought about it so much that you can't think clearly any more.'

She talked on quietly until the swollen lids closed over the blue eyes and the pinched, exhausted face relaxed. She smiled down at him; Joey was fast asleep.

Rowena sat holding Joey in her arms and thinking

about what he had told her. She remembered how Dugan's horse had been found still saddled and bridled, and of how there was no sign of the man. No one cared for him. Most people thought he had stolen a better horse, perhaps with the bridle and saddle, and in his callous way he had not bothered to unsaddle his old horse. Of course Joey must make a clean breast of his part of the business to his father for the sake of their future relationship. It would be up to Jim to decide on how much he must tell the police when he told them where to retrieve Dugan's body. She hoped he would be merciful to Joey and not stress to the police the part that Brumby had played in the man's destruction. They might well assume he had been killed ill-treating his own horse, or from a fall, and that subsequently the brumby herd had galloped across the plain, their hooves beating down the walls of the crevice and covering the man's body. On that lonely plain the body might have remained buried forever.

The woman's arms began to ache, and she realized with a start that it was dark not only on the verandah but outside as well. Geoff would be home soon. She meant to ask him to ride over to Jim's to say that Joey was with her, and to ask Jim to return with Geoff. She did not want Joey to go through another night without talking to his father.

Joey woke from his sleep. For the first time in weeks he woke happily, not weighed down by the dark cloud of guilt and fearful retribution that had filled his mind for so long. He went and washed his face and hands and then helped Rowena get the supper while he waited, a little apprehensively, for his father to return with Geoff.

When his father did arrive Joey ran out and stood uncertainly beside Trixie in the gloom. His father's friendly, casual manner reassured him, and he made a gesture that happened very seldom between them because Joey thought his father might think it sissy. He put up his small paw and held to his father's hand as they went indoors together.

Having eaten his supper Joey became tremendously sleepy again.. He struggled against it manfully. Rowena sent father and son out on to the verandah to talk. While they were out there she told Geoff everything. His only comment was, 'Poor little bloke.' Then Jim came through the doorway. In his arms he carried the heavily sleeping Joey.

'Can I put him somewhere, Rowena, while we talk?'

It was late that night when the two men and the woman came to the decision that it was possible and right to keep Joey out of the affair when Jim went to the police. For bush-keen eyes there must be some sign of what lay beneath the red earth, if a man looked closely enough and in the right spot. It was perfectly credible that so much time had passed since Dugan's death without his being found. Jim would leave it to the police to discover the identity of the body. No good purpose could be served by dragging either Joey or Brumby into the affair.

Rowena told Joey his father's decision, then she looked at him very seriously and said,

'You must never *ever* speak of what you saw, Joey. Your father and Geoff are doing what they feel to be right, but none of us know if those things are right in the eyes of the law. So now you must try to forget all about it.'

It was as Jim thought. The finding of the body, his statement to the police, and the identification of Dugan's body proved to be a nine-days' wonder. No one even thought of asking Joey any questions. It was surmised that Dugan's horse had thrown him into the fissure, that the earth had crumbled in on top of his body, and had been packed tightly by the movements of cattle or horses. After a couple of months no one spoke about it any more.

To Jim, Joey was no longer the little boy he had been before his terrible experience. He had grown up a great deal and he was graver, more thoughtful. In his heart Joey believed that he would still be punished for his belated confession, perhaps by the non-return of the brumby herd.

He found himself loath to go up to his look-out. The dreadful scene that he had watched enacted on the arid plain below was seared into his memory and he could not face looking at it again. Gradually Jim came to understand why it was that Joey never went now to look for his beloved herd, and his father worried about it. Jim did not want Joey to have any part of the land that he could not face. He spoke to Rowena, but she advised him to leave the boy alone.

Then one bright moonlight night, some months after the Dugan affair, Jim opened his eyes to see Joey's small figure dark against the white eye of the window. Something made him roll out of his bunk and go and stand beside the child. Joey did not move or turn his head as his father came beside him.

Jim looked out on the platinum world and there, glittering in light that seemed to curdle along his silver sides, was Brumby, moving quietly, head high, nostrils flaring, breaking into an easy, cadenced trot as he circled the stable which held Moonlight.

Jim smiled to himself. He supposed that this marked the end of his plans for Moonlight. He had been working on Joey to let him take the mare to the Larrakia stallion. Well, Moonlight was the boy's own mare, it was up to him to do what he chose with her.

For a long time father and son stood side by side listening to the soft shufflings and whinnyings, watching the quiet, restless movements of the stallion.

'Isn't he a beauty?' Joey whispered. Then to Jim's surprise the boy turned from the window and went back to his bunk. Jim returned to his bunk too, and for a long time he was conscious that Joey was still awake wrestling with some problem of his own. Jim went back to sleep and after a time Joey slept too. He had made his mind up, he would offer a sacrifice in his own way to atone for what he had done, for that thing which he could never quite forget.

The next evening when Jim returned from work Joey did not run to meet him as usual. Jim saw the small figure sitting on the step and he called, 'Hello!' and Joey called back to him, but still he did not go to meet him.

Jim put Trixie in the yard outside Moonlight's stable to rub her down. When he finished he turned her loose, and glanced into the stable as he always did. He stood looking thoughtfully into the gloom, then he turned away without latching the door. He walked quietly over to where Joey was and sat down beside him. After a silence he said,

'Why did you do it, son?'

'Because I don't believe that Brumby will ever bring his herd to the mountain corral again.'

Jim gave a restless movement, but Joey went on talking, his face grave. 'I let Moonlight go to him.'

Jim's eyes were puzzled and he asked again,

'But why – why? I thought you wanted to be a horse breeder and – well, breeding from Moonlight was your chance to begin?'

Joey looked down at his bare, brown feet and moved his toes in the dust, glancing obliquely at his father before he said,

'We never talk about my mother, but we did once before. Do you remember I asked you why you let her take me when you knew that she didn't want me?'

Jim nodded. 'Yes, I said I thought she needed you even if she didn't realize that she did.'

'You said something else too.'

'I told you that I was the strong one and that strong people have to make sacrifices for the weak.'

Joey nodded. 'Well, today *I* was the strong one. I knew that I could keep the stable door shut, or I could open it. So because I'm the strong one and a man' – his father smiled a little sadly, but Joey went on – 'I've given Moonlight to Brumby because I love them both so much and to make up for what I did – don't you understand?'

'I think I do. But still –'

'Don't you *see*, Dad? In a few years there may be a ghost herd of champions, hard and swift and strong, the way a champion has to be. Then we'll have fences and p'raps we'll be able to really go after them, you an' Bill an' Geoff an' me, an' we'll bring them back an' begin to tame them gradually – oh, don't you understand, I'm a breeder *now*?'

Jim gave a short laugh. 'You certainly are! I don't know where you get your ideas from.'

'I do. I get them from you, only you'll never let your ideas out. You don't think things'll happen because they're too far off, but I believe they will.'

So Moonlight went to run with the brumby herd. For a time they stayed in the scrub, and often, quite un-watched by human eyes, the great stallion would come a few yards from the darkness of the scrub and stand, his splendid body motionless, a white blur against the dark trees and the red earth, and look towards the mountain of his birth. He would begin to circle with his cadenced trot, shaking his head, flaring his nostrils, eyes wild, to pause and stare again towards where the sharp peak cut the indigo, star-pointed sky. The breeze came from the clean heights across pockets of sweet grass, so that the stallion reared his splendid head and called across the distance. But he never attempted to cross the red plain.

As was their wont the herd became restless, and Brumby led his sixteen or more mares and foals back into the wastes. There were changes of seasons, and some compelling instinct drove the leader back again. Chance brought a forgotten memory to him, a link between the colt that had fled with his mother from the mountain, and the matured stallion. Something kept him near the plain, and yet held him from crossing it to reach the sweet grass growing in the high places of his beginning.

Whatever sense brought Brumby back to his birth-place was dormant in his half-brother, Myall. Since that dreadful day when the whip-cracking and the hard-riding men had sent Myall and all the mares to follow the stream of escaping horses from which Brumby broke away with his mother, who was so soon to foal, Myall followed the herd and went farther and farther from his old home.

Then he was driven from the herd by the stallion who took Yarraman's place as leader, and the big white stallion, so like his half-brother, wandered about alone for almost a year. Then came the day when Myall, who was a fine beast almost as large as Brumby, fought his way back into the mob, driving away the leader, a dying king who did not last long after the battle for a supremacy he could not hold.

Myall lived and guarded his herd in the vast wild spaces of the north-west away from Brumby.

It was winter and frost lay hard and white on the ground when, for no concrete reason, Joey felt the stirring within himself of the desire to return once more to his look-out, to do what he had so often done on those nights that now seemed so long ago.

He waited two nights until the moon was full, then he pulled his old jacket off the peg and moved quietly out into the frosty night leaving his father sleeping.

The grass crackled and tiny javelins of frost pierced between his toes, but he went down the hill to where Flash made a dark blot against the whiteness. He slipped on the bridle and climbed on to his warm back, turning him towards the creek beyond which rose the mountain.

Like someone on a pilgrimage, Joey knew that the faith in his heart meant something it had not meant before. He knew long before his miracle happened that it was going to happen. He left Flash and climbed to his rocky perch, then he settled himself before he looked out over the plain that held such terrible as well as such sweet memories for him.

His eyes were caught by movement. As the Phoenix rose on fiery, red-golden tongues of flame as from a bed of naked sword-blades, so the silver horses that galloped on the plain seemed spawned from the cold fire of the moonlight. The child could scarcely see the two palely glittering shapes that raced and wheeled and raced again, except when they passed before the darkness of the trees that edged the plain.

Then, like the flash of swiftly crossing rapiers, in moonlight that made them unreal, remote, lovely, he saw creatures that seemed to lack the hot blood and fire of animal life and had become phantoms of the silver night – his phantoms, graceful, floating shapes, one much smaller than the other.

The greater phantom stopped, wheeled and stood facing the mountain on which the boy lay concealed. The fine head went up and the piercing challenging cry rang out. It was at once a salute, a demand, and a cry of victory. The small silver mare moved beside him, then from the darkness of the scrub, in answer to that cry, poured a mob of more than thirty brumbies.

Led by the swift silver horses they came galloping over the plain to the foot of the mountain and up the steep side, following the sure, remembering hooves of the stallion.

At last the boy lay on his stomach and looked down over the natural corral, filled now with splendid, vital wild horses – his dream come true. In the centre of the herd the great stallion lifted his head and screamed his challenge to the night. There was no answering challenge; he dropped his head and weaved his way through his mares. Brumby had come home at last.

Some part of every day or night Joey crossed the creek and went to look at his horses. For five months they had lived peaceably in the corral, sweeping across the plains at night. It was eleven months since he had let Moonlight free to join her mate, and early one morning Joey picked his way across the creek and towards the foot of the mountain. His naked feet trod the earth soundlessly. He stopped when he saw a faint movement within a copse of trees, and heard a soft, whickering noise.

Within the trees stood a silver mare, Moonlight, and Joey's heart leaped with joy. She had come towards him, towards her home in her greatest hour. Now she was making tremulous noises of love as she nudged a newly born, smoky colt to his feet. He stood swaying a little, his tiny hooves squared, his body still damp and his great soft eyes seeing the world for the first time as he lifted his little muzzle to his mother.

The boy stood, his eyes far away, seeing not only the new-born foal, but that same foal when he had become a long-legged yearling among a dozen others, all sturdy, enduring, beautiful, all herded within the new fence that formed a vast paddock surrounding the homestead. He saw himself and his father handling the colts; he felt the warmth of their bodies as his palms touched their silken hides. Then his eyes came back to the present and shone with love and triumph as they saw again the velvety symbol of his dreams.

'Florian!' he breathed with softness and love as intense as the mother's own. 'Oh, Florian!'

Joey stood for a little while lost in his happiness, then he turned and ran back home to tell his father.

If you have enjoyed this book and would like to know about others which we publish, why not join the Puffin Club? You will receive the club magazine, *Puffin Post*, four times a year and a smart badge and membership book. You will also be able to enter all the competitions. For details, send a stamped addressed envelope to:

The Puffin Club Dept A
Penguin Books Limited
Bath Road
Harmondsworth
Middlesex